The Trouble with

Harry Champion

by

Ian Harrower

ISBN: 978-1-326-77265-9

PublishNation
www.publishnation.co.uk

Chapter 1

Spoons

Some people live a lifetime and they never experience the blend of hurt and intoxication that can pour from a heart punctured by one of cupid's golden-tipped arrows. I had double entry wounds!

Two women loved me. Incredulously, I had landed the gig as the romantic interest and somehow I had become jumbled together with both the sensitive Rachel and the highbred Angelina.

At the end of a helter-skelter summer that twisted across 1998, my ping-pong shenanigans had been neutered, however. I knew enough back then to know that love wasn't just about how you felt about a person, but how you treated them. I needed to make a commitment.

All of this took place in the bewildering days before Google and so my decision had to be made without the guidance of the 1,660,000,000 replies to the search: *How do you know you're in love with the right person?* Today, it turns out that there are 344 million results to the search: *What to do if you love two people at the same time.* But back then, at the fag-end of the twentieth century, important decisions depended largely on intuition. There were three principle characters involved and equally culpable in this little closet drama, of course. But this is my version. I offer you a sort of pre-digital, old-school observation.

I loved Rachel. I loved Angelina. I really would rather have not been forced to make a choice between them. I could have carried on happily, living a life like some high-ranking French politician, floating between the two. This was a confirmation for me that love was no longer a binary choice; that love contained within its bandwidth a range of different, nuanced, emotional possibilities. We were not in France, sipping wine in a Parisian cafe alas, but in Edinburgh. And even though we were surrounded by that city's post-enlightenment New Town, its Georgian refinement, we were still in

Scotland: a small country at the northern edge of Europe that hosted short summers, really shite winters and where traditions and superstitions seemed to take a whole lot longer to thaw. Also, Rachel and Angelina were not very keen.

There are rules. There are myths and philosophies. And being in love comes with an instinctive cultural shorthand that centres on the concept that every person should find 'one true love'. Two thousand years of Western tradition and culture, from Shakespeare to Niffenegger, Elvis to One Direction, Mills & Boon to *Cosmopolitan* – all those hollow hearts hoping to find 'the one', a soul mate with a matching rhythm, some pre-ordained cosmic twin!

But before I get ahead of myself I need to provide a little backstory and attempt to untangle for you the emotional pot-boiler that I had found myself swirling around in with Rachel and Angelina. So I'll begin at the end and the morning that I finally made my mind up to take a chance with one of these exceptional women. In my pocket I was carrying a note from Rachel. She had delivered it to me a few days before and it contained her prayer that she and I would build a life together. Angelina had delivered her ultimatum succinctly, eyeball to eyeball, as was her way.

"Ditch the bitch and stop fucking me about or you're history!"

Chapter 2

Everybody Knows

I first met Angelina in the Barony Bar on Broughton Street, Edinburgh in 1993. It was an early summer's evening and I had been invited to meet Angelina by a journalist colleague of mine called Hugh. Hugh was an ink slinger who had rotted his teeth in the alcohol-soaked regional newspapers from Inverness to Auchtermuchty. He had been on and off the wagon more times than a Wells Fargo employee but always appeared to have his eyes open for a new experience. He had insisted that I join him to meet up with his neighbour and friend Angelina and listen to his latest pitch. My thing at that time was music journalism; I was a late bloomer in many ways, but I had managed to con my way onto the payroll of a popular weekly listings magazine where I spent my time reviewing local band demos, blagging my way into concerts and interviewing any musical celebrities who were touring in our parish. I supplemented my income with as many copywriting commissions as I could tease from a couple of local advertising agencies and I tried my best to sex up the brochure copy (websites were just beginning to be a thing back then) from steel fabrication to industrial paint thinners. I boasted one grey charcoal suit and a battered old briefcase. I had recently split from my childhood sweetheart, Heather. Our daughter, Haley, was four years old and had just started nursery school.

Hugh's elevator pitch, it transpired, was to establish a new business magazine aimed at entrepreneurs. There was a growing generation of people who wanted to follow Richard Branson and become tycoons. A worldwide web was emerging and opportunities were waiting along every megabit of the information superhighway. Hugh attempted to seduce us with the revelation that he had major investment backing. It turned out, on closer interrogation, that he frequented the same sauna parlour as a couple of pinstriped fund-manager types who toggled between London and Edinburgh. Hugh had secured no more than a 'Sounds good, let's get together and talk' commitment from his pals before they were escorted off for their weekly blowjobs.

Hugh and I had volunteered our observations about our small Northern European country on many occasions over a glass or two of single malt. We loved to debate and share our views about Scotland and its people, where she was headed on the eve of a new millennium. Drunk, we loved nothing better than to get all nostalgic whilst singing along to The Proclaimers and feeling equally mournful about the passing of the generations who had borne the brunt of economic reconstruction in towns like Bathgate and Methil. Linwood no more and all that!

I had a thing for Angelina from that first minute my eyes locked onto hers. She does have astonishing, deep, dark eyes, though. I never knew that I was an eye man. Ka-ching! Have you ever found yourself staring into someone's eyes and thinking, *God I fancy you*, but finding yourself politely talking about Scottish enterprise and the advantages of hot desking?

Angelina was exotic. Spanish or Argentinian genes. She held court. A lady who was comfortable in all strata of company. Animated, passionate, a fusion of posh-school privilege, sophistication and culture. Here was someone who lived the lifestyle that you read about in *Cosmopolitan* I imagined. I had an Angelina crush. Mind you, she swore like a lager-swilling sheep rustler.

Angelina occupied a stratum well beyond my coefficient at that time, but I sort of sensed a wee spark, a connection between us. I was deluded, I soberly reminded myself. I was currently untangling my life from a failed marriage. But what the heck; I could allow myself a wee blissful float and drift along the warm, turquoise waters lapping against the shore in my dream cove, before the cold slap back to reality and the uncomfortable recollection that I was sleeping in a one-bedroom flat on a mattress with no furniture.

My marriage to Heather had been decomposing for some time. We had been together since school. It had lasted nine years. We were sunk by the strain of a new baby and the growing tension between our income and expenditure. We robbed Peter to pay Paul then asked

Peter for forgiveness and then renegotiated our repayment terms with Paul.

I can look back now and just about remember my glowing nineteen-year-old bride. We were children dressed in grownup clothes on our wedding day. We set up a home, but unlike our cheap self-assembly furniture, marriage came with no instructions. Haley was born four years later. Heather, who had always been supportive and indulged my creative impulses, was suddenly in favour of a regime change. She craved security and stability. She wanted a provider. I no longer fitted the profile. There was a rupture at the heart of our mutual aspirations. We drifted towards stalemate, fading, disappearing and unwrapping.

There are three sides to every story, of course. Heather would probably maintain that I was an immature dreamer, frightened of responsibility. A useless cunt, basically!

Chapter 3

There's a Place in the World for a Gambler

We expend so much energy squatting in borrowed and inherited ideas of ourselves when we are younger, anxious not just about our outward appearance, but obsessed with seeking approval for gestures that we can graft onto our personality in the hope that these will help us make our way in the world. I guess that's why books with titles such as *The 7 secrets of highly successful, habit-collecting Samurai* prove so popular with striving people travelling through international airports.

In my late teens, a girlfriend once told me, "You know, Harry, I love chatting with you. You remind me of a big comfortable sofa that I can cosy up to." My role in my girlfriend's life wasn't that of 'Titan the Love Pistol'. Harry Champion was unthreatening, likeable, understanding. I spent many years colouring in those shapes of me and trying to fade my ambitions, dissociate my desires. As we grow older we discover great comfort in stripping away all the layers of nonsense that we have collected. The deepest joy is learning that we still care about preening, but we now have the confidence to face the world and present an authentic version of who we have become.

I shudder to think about it now, but I once earned a meagre living mis-selling insurance. My business partner was a friend called Philip Murdoch Hain. Philip had grown up somewhere posh in rural England and had attended a private school, rather like the Jennings character created by Anthony Buckeridge in the books I had grown up loving. Philip and I started at the arse end of the financial services industry. We were very similar to drug pushers selling on street corners and were in the sump of some elaborate criminal pyramid scheme. Those private schools majored in the importance of glittering prizes and beat that message into all those privileged little minds. Philip was so competitive about working leads, securing appointments and making commissions. He needed to win at everything. Naïvely, I had imagined that my amiable, witty disposition would attract sales because people would … well, like me? It was Philip who achieved sale after sale and raked in the cash and I pretended to be comfortable playing second fiddle and enjoyed countless cups of tea and interesting chats on mucky wind-skelped nights in the front rooms of modest terraced cottages in Coaltown of Balgonie.

I learned a valuable lesson about life and achievement in an enterprise, however – you must know exactly what it is you want to do and where you want to go. Winning only really matters if it's something you passionately want to win. Many of us spend long periods of our lives simply meandering off course and there is much that can be rewarding about a good meander.

Circumstance meant that I was able to continue to meet up with Angelina as the summer of 1993 developed. Our mutual friend, Hugh, and his idea for a publishing empire quickly dissolved, but Angelina and I found reasons to meet for coffee and somehow I scraped together the money to explore the city with her and its blossoming new appetite for places to lunch and dine.

There is a spot on the cusp of craggy old Arthur's Seat, which is our geologically friendly community volcano and where a couple can climb or park a car and take in a view across the rooftops of glorious Auld Reekie. I drove Angelina there one evening after she had accompanied me at a formal business event. Being a recent émigré from Fife to Scotland's capital city, I was untutored in the etiquette of these swanky occasions. I knew the very girl for the occasion, of course.

Around our table that night were some of the wealthiest and most influential men and women in the country. Angelina had no concerns about the company or the setting in the magnificent Signet Library and it was a delight to watch from my end of the table while she enchanted the accomplished men and ladies around her. She was young and bright, gutsy, opinionated and confident. She shared opinions about wine with aplomb, which hinted at experience of the finer things. They talked business and schooling and she matched them and clearly impressed them. I was overshadowed but happy to be swept along on her coattails. It was a privilege to observe a social butterfly at her most beguiling, living the life she had been born and educated into.

And so, in my car parked on top of a dormant volcano, we looked across the rooftops and the glimmering lights of Edinburgh and I pressed play on the CD player and Dan Fogelberg sang, 'There's a song in the heart of a woman that only the truest of loves can release.'

As Angelina and I laughed and reviewed the events of a most wonderful evening, I stretched across, kissed her lightly on the lips and said, "Thank you. I hope you find your song!" As I drove her home, I'm sure I could hear her heart melting.

I had been miscast as a comfortable sofa. I knew what I wanted and where I wanted to go.

Chapter 4

Waiting for my Real Life to Begin

We learned that our mutual friend, Hugh, who had introduced us, had fallen for a Spanish waitress and made the decision to take off for a life of rustic romance in the mountains of Andalusia. Angelina and I began to discuss the possibility of launching a magazine title of our very own. Angelina had the contacts in publishing and the experience with the business community. With financial backing, she could make a go of that type of venture. My contribution, and what Angelina valued most about me, was my creativity. I've always liked to create things, imagine something that's never been before, and I have been blessed in life that I have been able to manifest those instincts in a variety of ways. Angelina encouraged me in this and she was very good at honing my musings and making better commercial sense of them. So we began work on putting together a business plan and slowly, line-by-line, the concept began to take shape. It was a daunting prospect, however, brought home to me one day as I glanced along a newsagent's magazine rack. Staggering arrays of both general and specific titles were all competing for the apparent insatiable demand of the reading public. This was in the days before iPads and smart phones, you understand. People still read things, predominantly on bits of paper.

The privilege of working with Angelina and witnessing her take on a project, as I did over the weeks that followed, was a real education. She was driven, methodical and I discovered that attention to detail was very important to her. There were occasions where I had been tasked to research an area or aspect for the business plan, where I would just get bored, distracted, and I would make up things based on my own assumptions.

"Where did you get these figures, that percentage? How did you arrive at that conclusion?" she would challenge.

"It's a guess," I would sigh, tired and in need of a break.

"Sloppy and lazy," she would retort. She had inherited a very strong work ethic from her father and for her there was only one way to do a job and that was the right way. As someone who is more of an instinctive thinker, I sometimes found working with Angelina a challenge.

Anyway, after about six weeks of very hard work we had completed our business plan. We had put form to a bunch of ideas and inspirations and had created a document which purported to be our strategy to turn our dream into a reality. I was beginning to feel good about the whole thing and was silently congratulating myself for, if nothing else, helping to produce a damn fine business plan, when Angelina informed me that we needed to start work on a few other versions of the same plan.

"We need one plan to take to a bank that will back us," she explained. "In this plan the cash projections will show the business as profitable. Our first year sales projections will demonstrate a steady and healthy growth curve and we will include a managed proposal of cash flow, highlighting a maturity and responsibility by the business owners. Banks like that kind of thing."

"Aye, right, of course," I replied, scratching my head. "And what are the other plans needed for?"

"We need another plan to present to the development agencies and the local authority, as they have grants and soft loans available for new start-ups like ours. This plan will highlight the growth potential of the business, how many local jobs it will create, how it will make a major contribution to the local economy."

"Any more?" I asked, my initial elation beginning to subside.

"Yep! We need a plan to present to potential investors. Now, this plan will need to be slick because they will want an equity stake in the company in return for their funding – how we are going to build a healthy profitable company in just less than three years."

"Three years? Why three?" I asked.

"Because that's when we sell the company. That's how the investors will make a sizeable return on their gamble. This plan will show how we intend to flog the company off to a bigger rival after year three. Investors like that; it's called an exit strategy."

"Is that us then? Or do we require any other versions?"

"Of course."

"Of course? What else?"

"The most important one of all, which is *our* business plan, the one which we are actually supposed to use. Most of it is bollocks you understand, subjection, a wish list. At best it will point us in a rough direction that the company might head if all goes to plan, which it never will!"

I was exhausted keeping up with the twists and turns of this strategy. However, some weeks later we had finally completed work on each of our business plans and Angelina announced that she was satisfied. So we began the 'beauty parade', a long and difficult wooing of potential backers. I learned as this process evolved that the trick was to set the banks up against each other. Whilst in consultation with each of the banks, Angelina began sexing up the offers of support from their competitors and began to create the illusion that our business idea was a safe bet. This, of course, once the seed was planted, allowed her to drive the interested bank managers harder and secure terms that were more favourable to us. She resolutely refused to contemplate providing them with personal guarantees and I was instructed to shake my head dismissively if ever this subject was broached. When they asked, "Is this part of the funding in place?" she would smile and say, "Yes, that's covered," without blinking. Of course nothing was covered, but it seemed that nobody would make a commitment first, so they all had to be 'encouraged a little'. That's how Angelina defined it.

Within a month we had secured the support of a major bank and investment in principle from a group of business angels: a group of wealthy individuals who had put together a small venture capital fund and liked to dabble in promising new businesses. We also learned that we qualified for some grant funding from our local enterprise company and council. We hadn't secured all the funding we had been looking for in our best scenario predictions, but we had enough to launch the title and run for six months.

The business angels insisted that we take on one of their people as a non-executive chairman. This was no hardship as we liked the guy and he had a wealth of experience in the publishing business, not to mention a host of important contacts. The angel deal came with reasonable conditions; they would provide start-up funding and additional funds, dependent on performance targets. In return for their cash we signed away 40% of the company. But, as Angelina pointed out, 60% of something to us is better than 100% of nothing. They believed in us and were prepared to back us with their hard-earned cash.

So we had successfully negotiated our way over the first hurdles and now we needed to put our paper plans into practice. It had been confusing, making cash projections that we knew would be wrong, estimating the costs of sales, which would be higher than predicted, and funding requests that investors always cut in half anyway. However, who am I to point out such madness, a simple wee boy from Fife, surrounded by these great minds that are responsible for spending millions of pounds?

The offices of our new publishing empire opened in early April 1994. The launch date for the first edition of *Cock a Doodle Doo Magazine*, our unique concept aimed at the growing band of small business entrepreneurs in Scotland, was set for October later that year. We had a few months to sell advertising space, commission the journalism and photography and produce the first edition.

We became totally absorbed, living, breathing our new venture. As Angelina and I began to recruit staff, hire office equipment and get our first edition into production, there was very little time for a social life. There were nights when we worked so late that I couldn't summon up the energy to tackle the commute back to my own lonely flat in Fife. On many occasions Angelina would offer me her spare room, cook a meal for us and we would both arrive early the next morning ready to face the challenges of the day. Over those first few months we saw each other every day, every evening, we grabbed lunch together and often shared a glass of wine and a bowl of pasta in the evenings, and all the time thinking and talking about the magazine.

As a part-time dad I now had access to Haley every other weekend. This at least guaranteed me some time away from work. On a few occasions Haley and I would invite Angelina along to join us for a trip to the zoo or museum.

12

One evening, we were invited along to a business networking dinner: another black-tie event, loads of champagne, canapés and nervous, dull chit-chat. We met up with some of Angelina's friends and it turned into a night out, more drinks and a late club. At some point in the morning Angelina and I stumbled back to her flat in a taxi and, like every other occasion previously, I assumed that I would be sleeping in the guest room.

"Sleep beside me," she said.

"I'm a vulnerable, recently separated man," I replied. "Are you trying to take advantage of me?"

"Will you burn in hell if you sleep with me?" Angelina asked.

I smiled and decided, "I think hell can be negotiated but it may require some serious penance."

Friends would tell us they thought it was inevitable that Angelina and I would finally get together and consummate our long-running courtship. Of course, I had been attracted to Angelina from day one. I'm guessing my mixture of humour, intelligence and the similar things we cared about resonated with her in the end. She admitted to me one night that she was happier when she spent time with me than at any other time of her life. Now that we were working together, both single, we were free to explore a conventional relationship. We both entered this new and exciting phase with trepidation and were worried about how this might affect our working relationship and the prospects for our business.

I was drawn to Angelina, I was fascinated by her, but she was a contradiction. To the outside world she presented the picture of a modern woman, intensely motivated, energetic and focused. She was ambitious and competitive, with a great appetite for knowledge, achievement, power and control. On the inside, though, there was softness, tenderness, insecurity and a subtle spirituality. These two sides of Angelina went to war every day and, in those early days when our relationship was taking its first awkward steps, I was never quite sure which Angelina was going to show up.

A few weeks into our new relationship, we were lying in bed one Sunday morning when she asked me, "How serious are you about us?"

Suddenly the mood of our little cocoon was transformed. I looked into her eyes and saw a deadly concentration there.

"I'm happy, Angelina. I hadn't realised it before but somewhere along our timeline I fell in love with you." There, I had whispered the L-word. I must confess, I expected some slushy togetherness to follow, some hugs and kisses. But not Angelina. No, Angelina wanted more than a declaration of love; she demanded an action plan.

"I'm in my late twenties," she told me. "I don't have time to mess about any longer. I want to be married, to have children. I need to be with a man that wants those things with me."

"Is this your way of proposing to me?" I asked, hoping to induce a little brevity.

"I've never met anyone like you," confessed Angelina. "When I was off for the weekend recently with my girlfriend you were in my thoughts every day. I was shocked by how much I thought about you, by how much I longed for you, how much I missed you. I need to know that you feel the same way, though," she probed again. "I've had lots of relationships with men and I'm tired of the games, the lies, the power struggles, the hurt. I need to know that this time I have someone who is willing to give it a go, to stick with me, someone who won't run away at the first hint of trouble. I need a partner and I want that person to be you."

So, on that morning, we made a commitment together, to be honest, to be straight, to learn and support each other, and a day later I moved into her flat. The day after that she threw a toaster at me, the first in a long line of household electrical goods and implements that would wing and whizz their way in my direction, with precise aim over the course of my time with Angelina.

Chapter 5

I Hope You Dance

Angelina and I settled into our new life together and tried to find a rhythm that would accommodate our personal and professional lives. This was easier said than done as very often, if we had a domestic, as we affectionately referred to all disputes and which originated from our living arrangements, the fallout would be carried over into the office and would manifest itself during a meeting, often with our new work colleagues in attendance. Alternatively, we would both return home from work, late in the evening and over a snatched bite to eat, and would continue our post-match analysis of the business day. It was claustrophobic.

At the same time, I was learning how to become a part-time father. My separation agreement with my ex-wife had stipulated that I was allowed to have access once a week for a few hours after school and every second weekend from Friday through to Sunday. Haley was five years old then. It's hard but not impossible to build a normal relationship with a child when access is restricted. Options are limited on a dreich Wednesday in November and so McDonald's was often the venue, trying to cram a week of fatherly support into a few hours over a Happy Meal. Sorry, did I claim earlier that I was creative? I felt guilty and inadequate, so I would try to make up the ground by becoming a weekend adventure dad, buying endless presents and arranging surprise trips.

In the early days following the separation, Haley would ask, "When are you coming to live with Mummy and me again, Daddy?"

Both Haley's mother and I had sat down with our child to explain to her what was happening. I think the script went something like "Mummy and Daddy are having a lot of troubles at the moment and are arguing a lot, so we have decided that it would be better if we live apart from now on." Of course, when you're five years old, all you can think is, *Trouble for who? Why have you done this to me?*

That first Christmas after the divorce, I was allowed a two-hour visit with Haley on Christmas Day. It was a crisp, freezing cold morning as I stood on the doorstep of the house waiting for her and I could hear the celebrations of Heather's family going on inside. A family where once I had been at the centre, where last year I had been the Christmas Day chef, but now I was left to stand on the doorstep with the door closed in the freezing cold. Haley and I spent those precious two hours visiting her grandparents and after I returned her to her mother, I went on to spend the dullest ever Christmas on my own.

A few days after that first Christmas, Haley and I arranged a shopping trip. Little girls warm to shopping much quicker than boys I have noticed and Haley was anxious to spend her Christmas bounty at the local Toys R Us store. We had a great day together and as we drove home I remember looking round and noticing that she had a wee perplexed look on her face.

"What's up, bambino?" I asked.

"Nothing," came her standard reply.

"Are you sure there's nothing wrong?" I continued. After a few minutes, I noticed the glint of a tear as it rolled down her cheek. "Haley, what's the matter, darling? I love you, please tell me what's upsetting you," I pleaded.

Haley turned, looked at me as if she were assessing me and then sighed before delivering an emotional punch with all the force of Mike Tyson. "Why don't you want to live with Mummy and me?" she confronted. "Is it because you love Angelina too much and that you don't love us anymore?"

Of course, I tried to reassure her, to tell her that I loved her. I was still her Daddy, even though Mummy and I had decided not to live together. I remember pointing out at the end, when I felt she was beginning to be reassured, that things had moved on now and that Mummy had Malcolm, her new boyfriend, and Daddy had Angelina. Haley had a furrow on her brow. She was thinking and after a wee while she retorted, "Hmm, Malcolm and Angelina," and left that possibility hanging in the air.

Chapter 6

Don't Let Me be Misunderstood

Angelina was without doubt a passionate woman. She did nothing in life half-heartedly, in or out, no compromises. She was quick to temper.

I recall an incident one evening, following an extremely stressful week at work. We had some trouble at the magazine; a major advertising client was running substantial arrears. Angelina was chasing them daily for payment. A small business has little margin for error and we relied on prompt payment from our debtors to keep our little enterprise ship afloat. Now, Angelina, as I have said before, likes everything in her life to be ordered, particularly financial matters. That night, back at the house, we had a power cut. It was a freezing night and she lay on her bed sobbing, with the duvet pulled around her. All I could hear through the despair was, "I hate my life. I hate you and I hate this freezing flat. I mean, look at me. I'm nearly twenty-seven years old and what have I got to show for my hard work? What happened to all those dreams I had? I owe thousands of pounds all because those fucking bastard arseholes can't pay their bills on time." More sobbing, followed by great wails and sobs and cries.

"Angelina, darling, look it will be okay," I attempted to comfort.

"And tell me how will it be okay? Who is going to make it okay? Who's been the one on the fucking phone to them trying to sort it all out? Who's been the one pleading with the bank manager to give us an increase in our overdraft? Was it you? No, of course it wasn't you. As always it's all left to me. Nothing would get done around here if it were up to you. You are a lazy bastard and I hate you. No, I fucking loath you. I hate and loath you and I hate this useless fucking flat and I hate your fucking smart-arsed friends and most of all I hate those smug, cunt-faced wankers who owe us money!"

The alarm clock is violently thrown across the room at this point, followed swiftly by a bottle of water and a shoe. The shoe actually bounces off my head.

"Hey!" I shout out, rubbing my sore head. "I'm only trying to help!" And this sends her off on another tirade. The verbal attacks grow in intensity. Doors are slammed and a flower vase is smashed to smithereens. "For fuck's sake, Angelina! Control yourself! You're acting like a lunatic!" I scream at her, now frightened and angry. "If you hate me so much then you can go and fuck yourself," I rant at her. "I'm not putting up with this shit any longer. I'm tired of pussy footing around you, tiptoeing to avoid confrontation, letting you have your own way. I'm fucking as sick as you that these bastards haven't paid us, the only difference is that I'm not as stupid as you are; I refuse to give them the satisfaction of letting them ruin my life like this." Then I delivered the nugget, "I mean the answer to this problem is simple; we have no money, they owe us money and everybody will just have to wait till they pay."

She swings a punch at me and proceeds to slap me on the back of the head. I push her away, grab my car keys and make a dash for the door.

"That's it! Run away! That's your answer to everything isn't it! Run away! Leave me! Go on, leave me then if you have the guts. You won't be the first. I'm too difficult!" she shouts and then crumples into a heap on the floor like a rag doll, like a wounded animal.

How could I leave her lying there? How could I run away and abandon her? I returned to the room and knelt down beside her, scooping her into my arms. "I'm sorry, Angelina. I'm so sorry," I said. She rocked in my arms. We were both exhausted now, had expelled so much nervous tension and energy that now all we could do was hold onto each other, making promises and giving reassurances that we loved each other and that if we faced the world together everything would turn out fine.

Angelina would counsel me that when she would get uptight, when she went off on one of her tantrums, the best thing I could do would be to hold her, hug her, reassure her. My instinct when someone is attacking me is to fight back or run. I really gave it a go, though. I learned that there were certain words and phrases that would ignite the blue touch paper. The tone and pitch of my voice was important, as was my body language.

Angelina's temper was one part of her complex character and had many facets. Never frightened to express an opinion, I marvelled at how many times I sat at a dinner party with Angelina and completely disagreed with her viewpoint or her vision of the world. Guess what, though? I love that about her. She is an independent girl, a free thinker who never shrinks from expressing her feelings. Her opinion is essential for me, anchors me.

There is a line from the Martin Scorsese film *Shine a Light*, featuring The Rolling Stones in concert. Keith Richards is asked who the best guitarist is, Ronnie Wood or himself? Keith larks about and then says something truly memorable. "Individually we're okay, but together we're better than ten other guitarists."

Angelina and I, despite the outbursts, were a good team. She provided the practical support and I pitched in the emotional support. Angelina had become my closest friend.

Chapter 7

Something Changed

The offices of the business that Angelina and I ran were part of a complex that had been renovated from an old bonding warehouse on the waterfront in Leith. Ingrained with Scottish and Edinburgh's history, Leith Docks was still a working port, only the whaling and fishing fleets were long gone, replaced by upmarket cruise ships and sophisticated survey vessels. Evidence of the gentrification of the docks and the dismantling of an industrial past in the area was everywhere to be seen and warehouses that once stored exotic goods from all over the globe had become designer apartments for the upwardly mobile. There were Michelin-starred restaurants, cosy bars and shopping malls and yet Leith stubbornly held onto a distinctive character all of its own

I liked the location of the office and often, when my head was cobwebbed, I would take a wee stroll around the shore, as it was referred to locally, and pop in for a coffee at one of the many cafés. Angelina and I had acquired a Border Collie called Hamish around that time and he would come to work with us and sleep under the desk in between patrols. As part of these daily routines I got to know some of the other folks from the other businesses in the building. Pretty soon there was a vibrant social scene going on where folks occupying the same building would meet in the pub after hours and this is where I met Rachel.

Flame haired, Rachel came into my life drinking vodka and cranberry juice. She was tall and had a slim smile and big eyes. She touched my arm and I made her laugh. The touch felt important.

Over the next few weeks my friendship with Rachel grew. We would meet by accident at first, normally when I was out walking the dog and she would be taking a wee stroll herself after lunch. Gradually these meetings would become regular and we would both look out for each other. Rachel and her husband, Steve, both worked for a small computer graphics business, which they had invested their savings in and which had grown from two original founders to twenty-five staff in a period of eight months' rapid growth. Like all start-up companies they were hopelessly underfunded and cash flow was a constant problem. Although they were beginning to win bigger and more prestigious contracts, there was chaos every month as the owners struggled to pay the staff wages. Constant deadlines meant all of the staff worked long hours under highly stressful conditions. In addition, Rachel and Steve were at the end of their eight-year marriage. Money was tight and the pressure of work added a sense of hopelessness, like they were both trapped in limbo, their futures on hold.

Rachel and I connected and discovered that we could listen to each other. Over the weeks an understanding grew; we found gentle words of encouragement. In contrast, my relationship with Angelina was increasingly unravelling. We tried to insulate work from home, introducing a buffer zone on the way to work and the way back. The rules were that we weren't supposed to talk about work when we got home after leaving the office and the car journey was supposed to be the transition time. It worked to an extent as long as there wasn't a major crisis. However, we failed to find a dialogue, safe words that could prevent us from winding each other up and so our frustrations grew. Imagine having Alex Ferguson, the ex-Manchester United supremo, as your boss and also your partner. There were many hair dryer moments. I admired Angelina's tenacity, her drive and passion, but we conspired to create a working atmosphere together that was most often a joy sponge. I hated it.

At home the arguments became longer, heated and edgy. Even the crockery looked troubled. Angelina felt that I shirked some of the mundane responsibilities with the business, accusing that I let her take the strain to handle the shit while I only ever engaged when there was something fun on the go, new features and promotions. The detail of the follow-through, the delivery, she argued, didn't seem important to me. The endless balance sheets, the juggling of finances to ensure that everyone was paid regularly, were apparently of no interest to me. I failed to convince her that my stress was just as acute as hers.

Often, after these fights, she would fold like a little girl and beg me not to leave her. I felt like I was trapped between a rock and a hard place. I was beginning to realise that love isn't a constant connection. Sometimes the signal is strong and other times it fades. Occasionally you question whether the source has been terminated permanently.

We carry around this wide-screen director's cut, an internal movie that we stupidly measure our relationships against. String orchestras fade in and out of the soundtrack and the leading guy or girl always manages to deliver the right line, say the right thing. Reality never matches up. I was beginning to accept that there was no such thing as the right person. The one. We are all so incomplete, fucked up in our own unique ways. The trick might be in finding the companion whose own flaws equalise our own. Yin seeks Yang.

Angelina and I could simply not sustain the pressures on our relationship that we had been living through. I began to flirt with the idea that if we were to salvage our personal relationship then we might have to consider giving up the business. I had come to doubt that we could find a way of reaching a balance, where we could successfully juggle living together as a couple and working together as partners in a business. The trouble is that Angelina didn't see the world this way. Giving up the business to her would be admitting defeat, would mean surrendering a dream. Failure. For a girl who had grown up adoring her hugely successful, self-made father, my suggestion was a bitter pill to swallow.

It was the summer of 1998 and like every other self-respecting Scot I was gearing up for the World Cup to be held that year in France. Scots had an added bonus that year, aside from actually qualifying for a major tournament, as our team was to open the tournament with the glamorous opening game in the Stade de France in Paris against the world champions, Brazil. The match would be watched by a TV audience of 26.4 billion across the globe. As the excitement built to fever pitch, the whole office block made plans to watch the game in our favourite local bar. Kick off on the opening day of the tournament was due at 4.00 p.m., although many of us decided to hit the bar at lunchtime and give up on any pretence that we could work.

Predictably, Scotland lost after a brave display and after conceding an own goal in the dying seconds of the game. By the time the match was over we were all slightly the worse for wear as much alcohol had been consumed. I remember it was a lovely summer night and in my excitement I had quite forgotten that the dog had been holed up in the office all afternoon. I announced to the crowd that I had better take Hamish for his walk and Rachel, who was watching the game with us, offered to come along and join us. For a minute I held my breath to see what Angelina or Steve's reaction would be, but they both seemed to be more interested in the post-match analysis that was going on around them, and Rachel and I slipped out together.

As we walked and shared a few laughs, Rachel turned to me and said, "I've been hoping that I could get you on my own all day." Her words hung in the air and as my heart leaped I wasn't sure how I should respond.

"I know," I finally replied. "I look forward to our little meetings. I've grown really fond of you, Rachel, think about you a lot, keep wondering what would happen if we were both unattached."

Now this was clearly dangerous territory but, as I have said, the alcohol had been flowing all afternoon, so it kind of loosened me up. I had been aware of the chemistry between us since the first time we met really and, well, damn it; you just want to know for sure sometimes, don't you?

Rachel turned and faced me. "Oh, Harry, I feel the same way. God, I don't know what I would have done without you these last few months. Your advice has really helped me. The only reason I can face coming in here every day is the thought that I will have a few minutes with you to look forward to."

I have never been one for courageous moves with women, but if ever there was a time that a kiss was called for, it was now. I took her in my arms and kissed her. Rachel was a willing participant. I can't remember what we talked about during the rest of the walk on the way back to the office with the dog and our return to the pub. Nothing was said about the kiss or what that meant and I think, on reflection, it was just the manifestation of the emotions we had both been feeling over the last months. It was an acceptance kiss, a recognition kiss, a comfort kiss perhaps; a realisation that somebody out there in the world found you attractive, needed you to some extent; a secret kiss between special friends that didn't need to be analysed, cheapened or dwelt upon. We returned to the bar and joined our partners and continued as if nothing had happened.

Later that night, while lying in bed with Angelina, I think she questioned me about the long time that I had been gone with Rachel, but I dismissed her concerns, cuddled into her and said, "If I could live my life again somewhere else I would like to be born Brazilian!"

Chapter 8

Fearless Love

Scotland had just drawn against Norway in our next group game and Brazil had beaten Morocco. This meant that if Scotland could beat Morocco in their final game, oh and if tournament favourites Brazil beat Norway, then we would qualify for the last sixteen of the World Cup Finals and the later stages of a major tournament for the first time ever. So I was contemplating all the permutations. I had my World Cup chart out and was plotting our likely opponents, projecting what could happen and imagining scenarios that could lead us all the way to the final. The phone rang. Angelina answered and it was my younger sister. They were soon into one of their mammoth telephone conversations, putting the world to rights. I was not really paying attention to what they were saying but at halftime I caught a comment and quickly discerned that they were discussing my daughter, Haley.

"I mean, that's what the monthly maintenance cheque is for," I overheard Angelina say.

"Listen," I butted in, "all of this has been sorted out between Haley's mother and me. What business is it of yours anyway?" Perhaps not the proudest moment in my life and certainly an intervention that I could have thought about before opening my big fat mouth.

Explosion ensues.

"How dare you?" Angelina screams. "I'm talking to your sister actually and I will bloody well say what I like, to whomever I like. Bastard!"

The telephone was thrown across the room in my direction. Fortunately, it snapped back on its cord and a trip to casualty was avoided. The phone, however, would need intensive care. Doors were slammed. Actually, 'slammed' seems a bit of a poor excuse for a verb to describe what Angelina can do to a door when she is in a

25

temper. I have never been in an earthquake situation, but when she slams a door and she's angry I'm sure that it must register on a Richter scale somewhere.

She stormed through to the bedroom and I could hear various household objects being slung across the room. Suddenly there was a massive crash and the sound of breaking glass. I detected that this meant our alarm clock had just been hurtled into the bedroom mirror. I could hear sobbing.

Fuck it! I thought. *I'm getting out of here.* I attempted to make my way to the doorway, but she met me in the hallway and slammed me a punch right in the mouth. I was knocked back into the lounge. She came at me again. Slaps followed to my head, a hard kick to my shin. My arms were flaying as I tried to get hold of her. She connected again with a mighty fist, catching the sensitive part just above my ear. It really hurt and I was reeling and then, bang, I lost my temper, like a mighty tidal wave rising inside me. I stepped back, crouched and before I knew it was pulling my arm back, preparing to slam her one with full force, right in the kisser. Somehow, however, and I have no idea how, the fist stopped on the back swing. I hesitated.

"Go on, then, hit me!" Angelina screamed. I swear she was foaming at the mouth.

"No," was the only phrase I could form. I managed to push her out of my way and I ran past her, out of the front door and into the freedom of the night. I drove off into the summer evening, heading for God knows where. I just drove, I had no plan, I kept taking a series of left and right turns like I was operating by remote control. Finally, I was forced to stop the car in a siding and I opened the door and emptied the contents of my stomach. I was shaking. My head was in my hands and I remember sitting on that lonely siding in the dark. Tears came.

Sometime later, I can't remember how long, I drove back home. I entered the house and Angelina was sitting on the sofa with a cup of tea watching the television. I slumped onto a seat and she calmly looked over at me and said, "Have you come to apologise?"

A collection of snapshots, that's what these are, thumbnails to help illustrate what it could be like living with Angelina at that time. There were many occasions when we would laugh together, have great fun, enjoy romance, soft moments, memory-making sunrises and sunsets. It's a complex picture to try and paint. But this is the moment where Angelina and I ended or at least where we stopped the first part of our story.

Chapter 9

Over the Hillside

My life was metamorphosing, careering, spinning around me and yet somehow I had become estranged from the fat controller. I had set up a business with Angelina, which I no longer enjoyed working in. The strain, the tension, that I felt in my personal life was overpowering. A week later, after another crazy argument with Angelina, I told her that I wanted out. Surprisingly, we were able to sit down and over tea and biscuits continue one of the most rational, practical conversations in many months. Our drains-up session lasted six hours. We agreed that the strain of our relationship stemmed from the pressure of living and working together. We had tried and failed to stem the haemorrhaging with various first aid practices. We both agreed that survival required major surgery.

The next day, we went into the office early and set up a meeting with Rodger, our chairman. Rodger had been appointed by the investors to look after their share and oversee the business. We had grown to admire the man over the three years we had been running the business and he had become an important mentor for both of us.

We met with Rodger later that day and made the decision to sell the company. Rodger wisely gave us courage to look at what we were doing as a step towards the next chapter in both our lives. He advised us that we needed to radically pare back our spending and our overheads so we would become more of an attractive proposition for an interested suitor. Rodger could sense our disappointment but he told us, "Look, guys, you have achieved a great deal; you have launched a new magazine and established it and survived for three years. The brand that you have built up is now worth something. You have given it a go; better to bring down the curtain on your own terms than have somebody force you to do it at a later date."

We both left the meeting slightly more encouraged but with a deep sadness. It still felt like throwing in the towel, giving up. It smelt of failure.

Over the next few weeks, we set about implementing the plan we had devised with Rodger. This included making some of our staff redundant. As the magazine had grown in popularity we had recruited full-time administrators, a sales manager, graphic designers and a financial controller; we now needed to reverse this and make the bottom line look more profitable. Making staff redundant must be one of the most crushing tasks that someone who has followed a business dream is asked to do. In a small company these people were not just employees, faceless numbers; they were our colleagues, our friends, people we shared so much of our lives with. We paid off our creditors, we fiercely pursued our debtors and by the end of the month Rodger had informed us that a large Swedish publishing company, who operated a series of similar titles across Scandinavia, was showing interest. Apparently, it appeared that our wee operation in Scotland would fit nicely into their stable, similar market and size of country.

The train carrying Angelina and Harry finally came off the tracks on Friday the 7th of August 1998. Angelina and I had hung onto a friendship for five years and lived together for nearly three. It was finally time to let go.

I had found the experience of working and living together with my partner claustrophobic, smothering. I know that it works for many couples and families, and the experience can make their relationships and businesses stronger. It didn't work for us. Being in a relationship polluted what we tried to achieve together at work. Angelina accepted that we couldn't maintain things as they were. She told me she would move back to her parents for a few weeks and take things from there. The next morning, she packed her bags and left. It felt scary and at the same time exhilarating. Could this really be my opportunity to live independently for a while?

The phone rang and it was Rachel.

Chapter 10

This Mess We're In

So, this seems like a fine idea, Harry, I thought and wanted to poke myself in the eye. You end a relationship with a girl with whom you have lived for three years and arrange a date with another woman the very next day. Yes, this is the inspired brilliance that will see you safely move into your successful single life!

So, here we were, then. Less than twenty-four hours after Angelina had packed her bags, I was preparing for a date with Rachel. Okay, not strictly accurate; this wasn't a date, but I was now technically single, as was Rachel. I was content to play the game, though, and pretend that nothing had changed. I had met Rachel lots of times for a drink or a coffee, a wee chat. That's it then; this is no different from those past occasions, Mr Champion. Sort your head out. Play it cool. Act no differently and everything will be all right.

It was a glorious late-summer evening and Rachel and I met up for a drink. We ended up driving all the way to St Andrews in Fife, and Hamish, Rachel and I strolled along the West Sands. It was a most pleasant way to end my first evening as a newly independent, single man. I sent out a few telepathic, 'Do you like me?' signals throughout the evening and concluded that I was receiving a positive response. There was chemistry between us. I knew that we both sensed it.

There was no word from Angelina the next day. It had been forty-eight hours since she had left me. I had a strange ache, like a weight in my chest since the moment I had woken. I couldn't work out what that was: regret, anticipation or excitement about my new radically changed future. I busied myself for the rest of the weekend with sorting the house out. I made a start on separating our things and had to stop when I got to the CD collection.

The following week was swallowed up by business meetings and administration duties. Angelina called and left an answer machine message informing me that she was going to take a week's, maybe two weeks', holiday. She explained that she had updated Irene, her secretary, and that there were a few urgent work things I would need to pick up. Understandably, there was a subdued atmosphere in the office. Many of my colleagues were working their notices. There was a surreal quality to the place, but I got my head down and tried not to think about the future too much.

Rodger bought me lunch and I brought him up to speed about the change in Angelina and my relationship. He appeared genuinely surprised, but annoyed me when he said that he would call Angelina and arrange to take her for dinner. I only got lunch!

The news from Sweden was good. A meeting was set up and they were flying their people over the very next week. Rodger informed me that they wanted full access to all our financials and much of the first couple of days would involve them sitting in the boardroom with their financial director poring over our performance figures. Apparently, they also wondered if they could set up exploratory meetings with some of our large advertising clients without prejudice, and Rodger assured me that all of this was perfectly normal and part of the bum-smelling process. Rodger explained that selling a business was very similar to selling a property. One must give the impression that there were lots of other parties interested and that we were in no hurry to complete a sale. Indeed, he urged me to keep the staff informed of what was happening and remind everyone to put on a fine performance since, clearly, if the Swedes bought the title then they would need staff to run the company in Scotland. He then informed me that this might include one of the directors, i.e. Angelina or me.

"Won't they want Angelina?" I asked.

"Not necessarily," replied Rodger. "How would you feel about staying on for another couple of years if they made it a condition of the sale?"

I left the lunch with Rodger with a lot of scenarios playing through my mind. To be honest, I had relied on Angelina most of the time to pay attention in financial meetings, chiefly because I really have a mental block with figures of any kind. Anyway, I tend to get bored very quickly in meetings, short attention span. But it was clear from my meeting with Rodger that I would have to sharpen my game if we were going to pull off this sale to the Swedes.

Rachel worked next door in the neighbouring business unit, so she kept me company throughout the days, popping in for a cup of tea and a chat and offers to walk the dog. Our relationship was beginning to blossom and I confess that I looked forward to the times when she would appear. I wondered what she was doing, what she was thinking about when she wasn't with me, and I noticed that I had butterflies in my tummy every time I saw her. Rachel was still living with her husband, although she had told me they had separate bedrooms and she thought their relationship had become more like a brother and sister than a husband and wife. Steve was, of course, devastated that his wife had decided to leave him; you could tell just looking at the guy. He walked about with a permanent hangdog expression. I formed the impression that he felt that as long as she was around, as long as he had contact with her, there might still be hope that she would come to her senses and decide to make another go of it.

A new business opportunity meant that Steve was off to Cape Town in South Africa later that year. Their house was on the market and Rachel was in the process of finding a flat to rent. Steve was pleasant enough when we caught up, but I could tell he wished that I could be permanently removed from the planet.

Angelina finally called. She sounded surprisingly upbeat and together. She was very business-like on the telephone and asked for an update. As always, she barked out clarifications and wanted to know if there was any paperwork to back up any agreements I had made. Once the business items were covered, I asked her how she was doing.

"What's it got to do with you?" she replied curtly.

"It's got nothing to do with me, Angelina," I replied. "But I'm asking out of concern for you. We still have a business together, financial concerns and a history. I'd hoped that we could remain friends and, if that's not possible, at least act civilly with each other. If asking personal questions is out of bounds, then so be it. I'm wondering what our terms of reference are here?"

"Let's just keep it strictly business at the moment," was her considered reply. "Everything's too raw for me right now."

"How did your parents take the news?" I delved.

"Was there something you didn't understand about my last statement?" she fired back. "I thought the phrase 'strictly business at the moment' summed up my feelings on the matter succinctly. I can't think why you need clarification."

So with that we ended our first post-relationship phone call.

The evenings of those first weeks were taken up with visits from concerned friends who wished to lodge their support. There were lots of phone calls from family inviting me to lunches, dinners and assorted gatherings. My mother and father were particularly cut up, I could tell. They had liked Angelina, they thought she was good for me and were a bit shell shocked with the news that we had split up. They put a brave face on things, but, to be honest, they seemed more upset about my parting from Angelina than they had been when I told them my wife Heather and I were getting a divorce.

I had to break the news to Haley as well and that was a tough one. I kept getting the feeling that she was about to suggest to me, "For goodness sake, Dad, first my mum and now Angelina. Are you incapable of commitment? What's wrong with you?"

In the end, she wanted to know if we could still see Angelina and if Angelina would still take her horse riding.

Rachel and I went on our second date/outing together about a couple of weeks after the first date/outing. I had got tickets for a comedy show and the city was fat and bursting as it gorged on its annual culture feast – the Edinburgh Festival. After the show, we sat and ate ice creams on a bench in Princes Street Gardens, watching an Icelandic guitarist singing Irish folk music with an American accent.

Rachel stayed the night that evening and I woke up the next morning no longer a single guy. It was funny sleeping with a new shape beside me, a new smell, a different taste of kiss. Since that very first night we had met there was an inevitability that we would end up sharing a bed together and it felt good, like destiny had manoeuvred us together.

Chapter 11

Pavement Cracks

Rachel and I decided to keep our relationship secret. There was concern about the haste and how quickly things between us had developed. We were sensitive to the feelings of Steve and Angelina, although I'm positive that they would have put us straight that they required no sympathy from either of us and would have preferred honesty. There were further sensitive matters of unravelling the financial ties and, in both cases, Rachel and I had business as well as personal interests together with our previous partners.

So began a time of secret meetings, phone calls and stolen moments of passion. For me this added to the buzz. It was all very exciting really.

Angelina called, telling me she had met Rodger for dinner and that he had taken her to some swanky place in town. He had brought her up to speed on the latest news from Sweden and outlined some interesting scenarios for her. Basically, it would appear that he and the investors he represented had plans where they intended offering me to the Swedes as a creative director to maintain continuity in the new business if the sale went through. They had mapped out a different future for Angelina and wanted her to run a new technology venture. Most of the directors of this new company were boffins who had developed an exciting data storage application and powerful search engine. They wanted Angelina to become managing director, to organise them and put them on a more professional footing. It was a virtual company so they all kept in touch with each other from Amsterdam, Manchester and Edinburgh by email. It was clear that Angelina, freed from the stress for a couple of weeks, was feeling relaxed and beginning to enjoy herself. She sounded more like the Angelina I had fallen in love with a few years before.

My heart leapt a wee bit when she asked what I had been up to and I said, "Oh, this and that. Nothing special. Drinks with Joe, went to the cinema with Steve and Rachel and a few of the gang." 'The gang' referring to our drinking buddies at the office.

If women inherit an inner gift for nurture and nest-building, then surely one of the things that men are instinctively born to is lying and covering their tracks. Compartmentalising is our specialty. It's probably a dormant skill from the times when we had to go out hunting and pillaging. But there has never been a time when I have sat down with my friends and discussed the rulebook. "Right, lads, I have a wee misdirection issue that's causing awkwardness back at the homestead. Any tips for me?" Nope, you just sort of pick up pieces as you go and it starts early with us. "No, Mum, it was a big boy who done it and ran away!"

A particularly good technique is to tell versions of the truth. So, in the answer that I gave Angelina above, it was true that I had gone to the cinema with Rachel. It was untrue that her husband and our friends from the pub had joined us. But in this way I reasoned that I had nearly told Angelina the truth, which wasn't quite as bad as an all-out lie. I was hinting at something, which I could perhaps develop later, but was telling her nothing at the same time, covering my tracks as we hunter-gatherer types do – Grrrrrrrrrr!

If I had told Angelina that I had been doing nothing socially, I felt that she would have smelt a rat. No, this way I informed her that I was attempting a social life but at the same time had interjected a hint of remorse, wanting her to think that I was just so upset about our split that my angelic friends were spiritedly all gathering around me to help me through this painful adjustment.

"You're seeing a lot of her," Angelina snapped and for 'her' read 'herrrrasp' with a few tons of barbwire adorning.

"Who?" Sorry but you have to play the game don't you!

"Rachel!" snarled Angelina.

"Not really." *Shit, I've been rumbled already*, I thought.

"Well, you mentioned a lunch and now the cinema. Sounds all very cosy. Did anyone ask after me or were you all too busy enjoying yourselves?" asked Angelina.

"Of course they asked how you were. Actually, Joe mentioned that he would like to call you and arrange a drink." Master stroke; see how I did that? Joe, of course, hadn't even been part of the group that we had been discussing, but I had previously mentioned a drink with Joe. This was true actually, but then again, as my best friend and confidante, Angelina would expect this. Classic diversion tactic. Again, no doubt, some prehistoric pincer-attack thingy – genetic memory and all that!

"I'd love to meet Joe and go for a drink with him."

Result! thinks me. *You clever boy!* And then I think to myself, *Just how much would she like to go for a drink with Joe? Can I trust Joe? Surely I can. He's my best mate for goodness sake!* "Shall I get him to call you at home?" *The first skirmish*, I thought. *Not too bad.* A fairly dodgy and uncomfortable part in the middle, but I reckoned that I had successfully avoided a mega disaster for the moment. *Harry boy, you live to fight another day.* This hiding in the shadows malarkey was proving to be a headache, though!

Chapter 12

Through Your Hands

Angelina and I had rented and lived in a good-sized, three-bedroom basement flat in Edinburgh's New Town, which was ideally situated a short stagger home from the city centre. The flat had been our home for three years and it felt strange to find myself living there all on my own. But I began to settle into living like a single man, doing the things that I had always dreamed about, such as discarding clothing in heaps around the floor in the bathroom and bedroom, drinking milk straight from the bottle out of the fridge, playing music at levels the recording artists had intended and gloriously lying in bed and reading a host of novels with my own night light on till my eyes were so heavy with slumber that I drifted away. To be honest, there wasn't too much slumber actually. I was managing about three to four hours of sleep each night, but the trend was downwards. My mind seemed to be working overtime and even my precious fantasy football team, which had been a stress-relieving technique of mine for years, wasn't working. I started having a stiff dram before retiring every night.

I got a call from Lewis, a friend of Angelina's from her time in London, who had been a great friend to both of us over the last three years. I was touched that Lewis showed concern for me. In these situations, friends often feel that they have to display loyalty to one side at the expense of their friendship with the other party. Given that Lewis was one of Angelina's oldest and dearest friends, it made it all the more remarkable that he should take the time to give me a call and find out how I was coping. Lewis told me that he would be up in Scotland in a few weeks attending a wedding in Glasgow with Angelina and he wondered if he could fit in a visit with me.

I liked Lewis; he was a smart guy and I had learned a lot from him. He was the first openly gay guy I had been friends with and even though I pride myself on my liberal tendencies (I subscribe to

The Guardian at least every Saturday), I was amazed how I still displayed little pockets of inherited prejudice. For example, I remember an occasion when Lewis was visiting Angelina one weekend and I was taking a bath. Angelina and our guest had returned from a walk and on their return to the flat Lewis was bursting for a pee. I had just started drying myself down when he knocked on the bathroom door and asked if there was any chance he could pop in and quickly relieve himself. I'm not sure what I was thinking was going to happen, but I suddenly panicked and blurted out, "Will only be a minute." I think that the following sixty seconds is the quickest time in my life that I have managed to complete my ablutions and get dressed. As I say, small pockets of prejudice that still remained.

I was apprehensive about beginning a sexual relationship with Rachel, but also excited. We had no history. It was an opportunity to ditch some of my repression and insecurity. Life's training course for learning about sex for the average male isn't exactly Ivy League, filled as it is with half-truths and exaggerations by friends, firstly in the school yard and progressing in later life to alcohol-fuelled bravado in pubs. Oh, and of course pornography.

Like all forward-thinking men, I had read my share of *Cosmopolitan* articles and tried to memorise a few snippets of important information. There was a lot to take in, though, and we all know women are much more complex in their approach to sex than men. I remember taking a couple of golf lessons in my life and having sex with a woman is very similar. In golf, in order to hit the ball from the tee, you have to remember to grip the club with a special golfer's grip. You stand with your feet apart, your left leg at a right angle with the ball. You have to keep your back straight and your head up, your eyes on the ball at all times. Then you must remember to keep your weight on the right leg and swing the club back, slowly gathering tempo before returning the forward swing, keeping a smooth and open motion, hitting the ball on the upstroke and always remembering to follow through. Learning a few decent moves when it gets around to sex is very similar to mastering the intricacies of the game of golf. We have to remember that foreplay is essential. We have to seek out strange parts of the body called erogenous zones and, as the articles in *Cosmo* and other magazines are always pointing out, these are not always situated in the first three obvious places you would think to look for them. They can be on the ears, the back of the neck, the inside of arms and thighs. Every woman is different, of course, and there are no short cuts. It's not like you can nip down to the local sex shop and buy yourself an erogenous zone template and whisper to your wife or girlfriend just before sex, "Any chance you could slip this on, love, just till I get better orientation on your erogenous locations?" Maybe you can. I've never actually visited an Ann Summers shop, but such a product would represent a damn good idea if you ask me!

After a suitable period of mutual foreplay, we then move onto the actual main course, as it were, and there are encyclopaedic volumes of reference material available on how the act of congress can be carried out, spiced up, made more pleasurable and even spiritual. There are G-spots to be encountered and figured out, timing and numerous positions to be circumnavigated, and the constant worry for the male that he might reach a conclusion too soon or that he may suffer equipment failure or that his tackle isn't grand enough. And, if all of that isn't enough to agonise over, there is the warm afterglow to be endured, where the woman unwinds slowly and the male must fight his natural instinct to curl up and sleep.

Like the first few times I tried to hit a golf ball, I found that I was so busy trying to concentrate on all the things to remember that I would invariably miss the ball completely or it would go careering off in the opposite direction that I was aiming for. Sex is very similar; trying to remember all of those top tips, recall all the important snippets of information in an attempt to be a satisfying and innovative lover, sometimes means that we males fuck the fuck up!

Now, in this matter, I think it is safe to say that lovemaking is easier for women than it is for men. The expectation is on us to be expert lovers, to make the moves in bed, to know what we're doing. Like everything involving women, they are so much more complex. Males have been handily designed so that their erogenous zone and G-spot and everything else they require to be satisfied are all handily administered from a central hub. Being ruled as we are by a dictator means that we don't need to worry about power sharing and devolution to other parts of the body. Most of us, from the early ages of puberty onwards, become expertly adept at bringing ourselves to a satisfying conclusion.

Angelina was a great teacher for me. She was very communicative and, despite the fact that I had been married for eight years, I rapidly discovered that I still had a lot to learn about women's needs. Being with a woman who wasn't frightened to let you know what turned her on was a great revelation and I became a very willing and eager student. We could have shagged for Scotland when we first got together and even towards the end of our relationship I think it is safe to say that we still enjoyed a healthy sex life, if not such an Olympic one. I felt really comfortable and at ease with Angelina; we had been together and seen each other every day and night for a period of three years. I reckoned that represented a very high concentration of relationship and was probably akin to an eight-year relationship in normal circumstances.

As I embarked on a sexual relationship with Rachel, I was very eager to put what I had learned from Angelina to the test and see how I measured up now that I was operating in an open market, so to speak.

I came out the blocks quickly on our first occasion, determined to show Rachel my best moves. Instead of reducing her to a quivering jelly, though, I think that I confused her. No sooner had I begun to get a positive response in one area, I was off to another part, trying to demonstrate variation and prove that I was innovative. In the end I collapsed, defeated, having bored the poor girl rigid by asking her every few minutes for progress reports. There was an embarrassed silence as we lay in the dark afterwards. After all the chemistry that had been building up for months between us, I think we were both expecting fireworks. We would have settled for a sparkler twenty minutes in and, by the end, the reassurance that we at least knew where the blue touch paper was. To make matters worse, in the post-coital reverie, I had experienced a massive panic attack and had become convinced that Angelina was going to make an appearance at the door and catch us both at it. Try as I might, that image just refused to budge itself and I practically pushed Rachel out of the door and into her taxi home.

Still, practise makes perfect and if at first you don't succeed ... I wondered, though, after her experience, if Rachel would be interested in trying again. I had behaved really badly by trying to bundle her out of the flat. I pretended that she may not have noticed and that my stumbling around might be forgotten, forgiven.

I met Rachel for lunch the very next day and was just settling down, thinking that I may have got away with things, when she halted my optimism abruptly.

"You couldn't get rid of me quick enough last night. Was I such a disappointment?"

So much for subtlety then! I had been rumbled. I decided that there was no other option than the truth. "No, you weren't a disappointment, Rachel. In fact, there was only one person who was disappointing last night and that was me. Listen, I'll tell you the truth. I had a severe panic attack before you left last night. I know it sounds stupid, but I got this picture in my mind that Angelina was about to knock on the door any minute. It was such a powerful premonition, or so I felt, that I just went into spasms, fell to pieces. I felt for sure that she was going to walk through the door any minute and catch us both. I'm very sorry that I treated you abominably and can only hope that you can forgive me. It's all new to me this kind of thing, hiding our relationship in the shadows, hoping we won't be discovered. I'll understand if you want to cool things off for a while."

Rachel grabbed my hand, looked me in the eyes and said, "I understand. Listen, I had Steve asking me all morning what I was up to last night, how come I came home so late. He's been sticking to me like glue since we got up this morning. I'm sorry I was so abrupt there, Harry. I guess I just needed to hear that you were still interested in me."

So the lunch ended positively. We had faced out first challenge together, discussed it, shared our feelings and now we had moved on. I felt reassured, but at the same time apprehensive about the situation that I had created. On the one hand, it seemed stupid to entertain the beginning of a new relationship and accept the pressure from all sides that we were under. Why couldn't we boldly declare to the world our relationship? Rachel had told Steve that their relationship was over and although they both lived together, he knew that she was looking for a flat to move into. He knew that she wanted a divorce from him. What did he expect she was going to do, live like a nun?

Angelina was the same. We had ended our relationship. She had moved out, was getting on with her life. Sure, we had business and financial matters to work out, but why was I anxious not to come clean and tell her about my relationship with Rachel? I was wimping out. She would have to be told sometime. Would it make it any easier for her or me if I told her at some point in the future or I told her now?

Emboldened by my own reasoning, I returned to the office, having made my mind up that Angelina would have to be told the truth. I would simply get down in the foxhole, keep my head down and sit the barrage out, hoping I would survive.

Chapter 13

Protection

Angelina informed me on the telephone that she was coming over that weekend to collect the remainder of her belongings. Once again she was very friendly. She informed me that she had signed up for some stress and anger management sessions. She was enthusiastic about how they were helping her relax and she was buzzing about her meeting with the directors of the new technology company that Rodger wanted her to manage. I decided to put off telling her about Rachel, reasoning that I should really have the courage to break that kind of news straight to her face.

My best friend, Joe, called for me and we made plans to head off on a boys-only adventure to deepest darkest Newcastle – a weekend sabbatical tradition that we arranged every year. Rachel also called, saying that she was going to Wales on business in a week, which coincided with my recently planned trip to Newcastle. I went to bed that night feeling more positive that I may be able to craft the independent life that I had coveted for years after all.

The Swedish contingent arrived and set up camp in our offices. Angelina, Rodger and I, together with Simon, the company lawyer, were all there in our finest, smiling to welcome them, and I was tasked with giving them a walk through, familiarising them with *Cock a Doodle Doo Magazine* and introducing them to the team who, to be fair, were doing their bit to look like a positively motivated workforce.

After a day of meetings and then dinner, I got back to the flat very late. I was shattered and hoping that I could get some sleep that night. Joe had urged me to make an appointment with my GP and chat about prescription sleeping tablets. I had heard so many things about the side effects, though, that I decided to postpone that course of action, hoping that things would right themselves naturally. I had been under a lot of stress and concluded that once the deal with the

Swedes was done and dusted my sleep patterns would settle back to normal. Sleep deprivation takes its toll, though, and I found it hard to concentrate at work. I required more and more breaks throughout the day and was drinking alarming amounts of black coffee. Indeed, I felt so tired and rundown that I had been introducing a small afternoon nap to my routine. Now, clearly, I understood that this was a dangerous precedent, but I couldn't stop myself. I found focusing on a work task difficult. There were a few deadlines that were overdue, which I reckoned I could rescue. I discovered an email from a promotional client that had been decomposing in my inbox for a couple of weeks and I had no idea when I had last checked my personal finances. I knew that I had been abusing my credit card. I was running out of clean underwear and desperately needed to do some laundry. Back at home, I could no longer see the sink for a festering pile of dishes. The house needed cleaning, but I was so knackered. I needed to sleep.

Knowing that Angelina was calling that weekend got me fired up to attack some of my outstanding chores. I got to work and gave the house a fumigation. My laundry was bundled into black bin-liners and conveyed to my local launderette, where I discovered a very nice lady who sold me a service wash for only £4.50. I worked late into the night and felt that I began to regain control of the office. I was pleased to complete the day with not only a tidy desk but an organised filing tray, a task list and an empty email folder. I had arranged meetings that needed to be arranged and generally went home feeling like a proper entrepreneurial fire-wire, exhausted but lifted by the thought of a bath and clean sheets.

A few days later, Rachel and I managed to grab a night together and I cooked dinner for her. We had a relaxing evening and shared a bottle of wine. We snuggled down after dinner with some candles and soft music and she complimented me on how clean the house looked. I felt all self-sufficient and, fuelled by the wine, things got a little frisky. We were both keen to erase the memories of our first time in bed together, so we quickly retired to the bedroom. I felt much more relaxed that night and paced myself, no longer anxious to prove that I was a stud-muffin, but grateful to be enjoying such close intimacy with someone I really cared about. As the months of our friendship and our affair had passed, I had become very fond of Rachel. She was soft and sweet and fragile. She needed someone to look after her and when I wrapped her in my arms she could fit snugly into the space in the middle. That night, we finally had some fireworks; we lay in the dark and Rachel shuddered to a climax. Our lovemaking was soft and gentle, sleepy. I held her and felt tears on her cheeks.

"What's the matter, darling?" I asked.

"I'm just thinking. I can't remember a time when I felt this happy," she said.

Angelina arrived early on a Saturday morning and she seemed impressed by how tidy the flat was. Unfortunately, she didn't appear to be impressed with the contents of the fridge or the long-term prospects for the house plants, so I lost a few points. Hamish was, of course, over the moon to see Angelina again. To be honest, I had been so caught up in myself that I had had little time to think about what Hamish must have been making of all this. He seemed happy enough, but you can never tell, can you?

Angelina suggested a walk, explaining that she wanted to chat to me about a few things. It was a lovely morning so, after a cup of tea, we all set off. Hamish looked excited to have the family all back together again. Then again, Hamish was a bit of a tart and looked excited and happy every time someone offered a walk.

"I've been reading a really fantastic book," declared Angelina. "I'd like to share some things about it. It's really helped me understand what went wrong with our relationship. I've brought you along a copy and I would like you to read it as well."

"What's the book called?" I asked.

"It's called *Men are from Mars, Women are from Venus*."

As we walked, Angelina provided me with a brief outline. The author, who is some American doctor called John Gray, argues the premise that if we think of both sexes coming from different planets, men from Mars and women from Venus, we can begin to understand that we have very different cultures and perhaps, by thinking in this way, we can learn to understand each other better and work out a better relationship. As Angelina enthused about what she had learned from the book, I had to conclude that it sounded very interesting. The fact that we men like to fix things is interesting, versus a woman's need to share her feelings. It has been a source of bafflement to me throughout my life that a raging argument can develop in your relationship when all you want to do is help. I am also fascinated by the way they award points. Clearly this is a book that I should sit down and read.

When Angelina gets involved in a project it seems to consume her and this book had become something of a project for her. We sat down to take a rest at one of those wooden picnic benches and tables and she continued with her summary. It occurred to me that I might not even need to read the book. Angelina had consumed the thing from cover to cover and her summary was so good that I was sure I could go out and talk with confidence about it.

"The thing is …"

I became aware that Angelina was talking to me again.

"There are many male traits in the book which I think that I possess and many female traits which I think you possess. It's like in our relationship, sometimes there's been a role reversal."

"That's my strong, well-developed feminine side," I joked, but then I realised that it was okay as a joke, but I wasn't so sure I liked where this was going actually.

"In my usual way, I've tried to smother you, have been too much of a control freak to let you have the space to express your opinion. You're such a nice person, Harry; you're always trying to keep everybody happy. You have so much bloody energy to keep up that persona and that's because it's not just a persona; you really do have a caring heart; you really do want everybody to feel good about themselves."

Actually, I think I'll read the book after all; I'm beginning to enjoy this now.

"I've smothered you and bullied you and not allowed you the space and freedom to develop and grow in your own way. I realise that now after reading this book." There were tears in her eyes now. Angelina was so passionate about things. She had the most wonderful deep-brown eyes, though, soft skin and wonderful soft, dark-brown hair. I stretched out my hand to touch her cheek and she

46

covered my hand with hers. Angelina gave a little smile and said, "Sorry, I'm getting all emotional now and I promised myself that I wouldn't do that. I miss you, Harry. Really miss you. God, it's like something has died inside me. I've never ever felt like this before, never allowed myself to get so close to someone like this before." Pulling herself together, she stiffened up and released my hand. I sensed that something had transferred between us. "All I want you to do is read the book. I know you need time to be on your own, to work out what it is you want to do with your life, but I want you to know that I love you, Harry Champion. You are my soul mate and I can't imagine being with anyone else in my life apart from you. I'll wait for you. Take your time, there's no pressure."

I decided probably an hour or so before, when Angelina got into this conversation, that I wouldn't break the news about Rachel to her after all. It would be cruel and insensitive I felt.

The rest of the day was taken up with systematically stripping the flat of Angelina's personal effects and reaching compromises about jointly owned stuff. By late afternoon we had amassed a pile of cardboard boxes, which were taped down with notes itemising the contents. This is a very Angelina thing to do. It hadn't been all plain sailing and worry-free. She had flashed her temper a few times at me, frustrated by my inability to pack a box properly.

We discussed some financial matters. I told her that if I could I would like to be able to stay in the flat and take on the tenancy. She told me that the bank had requested an update meeting with them at the end of the month and that our business overdraft had risen substantially.

"We really need these Swedish guys to come through with an offer quick," Angelina says, ratcheting up the stress. "I want to be able to meet the bank manager at the end of the month with a firm offer to show him. That's our target, Harry. We have three weeks to sell the company. I want out now, want to get on with a new life. I'm bored with publishing." The rest of the time was spent talking about private finances, joint bank accounts and there appeared to be mountains of papers to sign.

She then started in on outstanding issues from the office. Have you done this? Have you done that? Finally, she revealed, "I got a call from Barry Brent at Easter Executive; he tells me he's waiting to hear from you about an October promotion. You need to keep on top of things, Harry. This guy is one of our biggest advertising clients and the Swedes may wish to talk with him. Get it organised!"

The tension is rising again and I can see that she is getting stressed.

"I'll call them on Monday," I say. I'm bored with this now and am beginning to feel the old tension rising inside me again. Sometimes Angelina can make me feel like a schoolboy giving an account before a headmistress. Of course, I realise how important Easter Executive is to the magazine. To hear her talk you would think that I float around all day in a daze. Once again, I think to myself that Angelina is the only one who thinks she has the right to get stressed about things. I have been stressed and worried as well; it's just that we manifest our stress differently. I've been in my cave thinking about things, pondering. Bloody hell, she may have read that book, but she hasn't really taken on board some of the crucial factors in it yet.

I return to the conversation to catch, "As I see things, you have enough cash in the bank to survive another month; after that you're going to struggle. You will have to pay the rent all on your own, your child maintenance. We have the car payments, which we need to discuss. Get it together, Harry. You need to get off your arse and get things moving; otherwise you're going to bring us both down."

Angelina headed off not long afterwards. I'm not sure if I listened to her final summations. I felt depressed, lonely now. I've never been one who wants to prove someone wrong when they criticise me. If someone tells me I'm stupid or lousy, I don't get all fired up thinking, *Right, I'll show you*. I just seem to fall into a walking slumber and think to myself that I'm stupid and lousy. Encouragement and praise are my motivators. Once again, after a session with Angelina, I had been left feeling browbeaten and worthless. How had the day started so optimistically and ended in such a downbeat fashion?

I made myself a cup of tea when she had gone and walked about the flat noticing the spaces on shelves where her stuff used to be. It all seemed empty now, the holes where Angelina's gear used to be representing the emptiness in my life. Still, it was Saturday night and I was a single man (well, nearly). Surely there was something I could arrange that would bolster my spirits. I had friends, both male and female; surely I could muster up something.

I knew that Rachel and Steve had some sort of family reunion thing going on that night, so dismissed the thought that I might meet up with Rachel later. I sat down by the telephone and started to make some calls. Joe and his wife were having a dinner party with some friends. Joe extended an invitation, but I didn't fancy playing gooseberry. I thanked him for his kind offer and told him that I fancied getting drunk actually. I called my mate Simon, whom I hadn't seen for a while. Again, he and his wife had arranged a dinner party. He had prepared one of his legendary curries. "It would be fantastic to see you," enthused Simon. I was tempted by one of Simon's curries, but I declined.

I went through my call list and realised that everyone I knew had made plans and were doing something that night. Well, I'll enjoy a night in on my own then, I figured. I drove to my favourite Italian on Leith Walk and ordered up a giant pizza (family-size pepperoni) and hired a couple of videos. Yes, you may mock from your digital streaming, multi-device podium here in the twenty-first century, but that's how we did it back in the day. Back home at the flat, I settled down and even allowed Hamish to snuggle in beside me on the sofa while we gorged ourselves and watched the movies.

Rachel managed a sneak call late at night and we talked for a wee while, which cheered me up.

"What did you do tonight?" she asked.

"Oh, Hamish and I had a lads' night in, you know. A few beers, pizza, couple of mucky videos."

Chapter 14

Dirty Little Secret

What difference did it make whether I had a relationship with Rachel or if I had run off with a Nepalese maiden? I was struggling with the half-truths and the lies, concerned about dislocating my soul. My expanding web of falsehood would perhaps build up like a cosmic plaque, I thought, and one day I might come to a point where I no longer would be able to distinguish the truth. Also, I reckoned that I wasn't very good at lying. The smart money would bet I would be busted sooner or later. Edinburgh is a village. Angelina, I was determined, must respect our new status and that I was living my post-Angelina life. If she flipped and decided to excommunicate me, so be it. The truth would bubble to the surface eventually, for certain, and it would be fairer that she heard the news about my involvement with Rachel from me.

Enter our mutual friend called Sarah. It had been a while since we had all been together. I bumped into her one afternoon while walking Hamish and we got together a few nights later for a glass of wine and a catch up. Sarah, Angelina and I had all known each other for years and as we settled down with our first glass of wine, Sarah was anxious to discover what had happened between us.

"Angelina has been calling me and leaving messages on the answer phone. I feel lousy that I haven't managed to see her, but I've been in Switzerland with work a hell of a lot and I've never had a minute. I can tell she's upset, though. So tell me. What's been happening?" Sarah delivers this and then curls her legs up under her. Nothing better than a good bottle of wine and a juicy bit of gossip to make for an enjoyable evening.

After another sip of wine, I began to summarise what I had been up to, including the ending of my relationship with Angelina and the start of my affair with Rachel. If you want to keep a secret, keep it to yourself is the golden rule, but that night I poured out all my troubles to Sarah.

On a good day, we like to consider that our friendships can be measured in absolute terms. Friends you can trust. But life and experience has taught us differently, hence the golden rule about keeping secrets. In that second that you let go of your secret, you pass over a precious key to your confidante, a key that you hope they will equally treasure as important. You have invited another to make a value judgment about how important that secret is and therein lies the rub. We all have an image of what we are like, how we are perceived by the world, especially by our friends and family. It is fair to assume that the image we have of ourselves is skewed, biased and therefore the people closest to us will probably have a better overall picture of what we are truly, consistently like. This is the basis for all those personality tests that you are invited to take. Through the act of sharing a closely guarded secret with a friend, we assume that the particular friend views you and the world in the same way. Dangerous assumption, for the reasons previously outlined. We assume that the friend shares the same values or at least values pertaining to sharing secrets. However, by sharing a burden or a secret, we download part of the problem to our friend. The friend will, no doubt, being a good friend, try to help us solve our problem or provide a sounding board for us to develop how we may solve our problem. However, what's that line about being a legend in your own lunchtime? Once the problem is in the public domain it can never be as precious to your friend as it is to you. He or she can't possibly feel every eon of emotion that you have invested in the challenge that has been troubling you for days, weeks, months; it's crazy to think that they would.

Then, of course, you need to consider if the friend you have chosen to share your most intimate secret with is married or has a partner or another best friend. Chances are, by sharing your secret with your friend, you are also sharing your secret with the partner or another friend. How well do you know the partner, the other friend? So by sharing your secret you run the risk of your secret flying free, out of your control. Of course, the partner or the other best friend will have a partner or a best friend and before you know it, the burden that you thought was most intimate to you is the subject of the office gossip, the pub debate or the hairdresser's salon. My point is that we all know that your secret today is tomorrow's gossip. Unless you're friends with a bunch of MI5 agents then I suggest you think long and hard about sharing your secrets with your friends. They are great people and all, but the temptation is just too much for them. Back to that golden rule – if you want to keep a secret, keep it to yourself!

So I shared my secret with Sarah and, a couple of days later, Sarah passed it on to Angelina. Predictable really! Sarah had arranged lunch with Angelina and apparently, depending on whom you believe, the meeting went something like this:

FX sounds of busy café/bistro

Sarah: So how are things?

Angelina: Not bad. It's been a tough couple of months, but I'm getting on with things. Lot of exciting opportunities on the horizon, so trying to stay positive.

Sarah: And what's it like living with your parents again?

Angelina: Difficult! But they've been really nice to me. I've set up an office in the spare bedroom. Mum has lunch ready at twelve thirty on the dot. I log off at twelve thirty and join her for a wee cup of tea and a sandwich and we watch the lunchtime news together. Of course, the laundry fairy visits regularly. I put things in the laundry basket and a day or so later things arrive clean and ironed in the drawers. That's a real benefit of living with your parents again.

Sarah: Lucky you. So have you been in contact with Harry? How are things between you and him?

Angelina: I'm really worried about him actually. I don't think he's coping on his own very well. He's been acting weirdly, trying to impress me, but I can tell that he's distracted. I've called him a few times in the afternoon and I'm sure he's been sleeping. The business is close to being sold to a Swedish publisher and I've left Harry to get on with it, quite frankly. Anyway, I went up to visit him last week and we had a long chat. I've been reading a book; you really must read it. It's called *Men are from Mars, Women are from Venus* by Dr John Gray. Oh, Sarah, it's been a revelation to me and has really helped me understand what's been going wrong with our relationship. We spent the day chatting and I shared with him a few things that I'd learned from this fabulous book. He seemed really interested. I think he just needs time to sort his head out. I'm confident that he loves me and we'll get back together soon.

Sarah: Did he tell you that he loves you?

Angelina: He said that he will always love me. I mean he practically calls me every day. I think he realises that he's made a mistake, but, you know, it's male pride. He wants me to know that he can fend for himself, negotiate this deal to sell the business and prove to me that he's this top entrepreneur. Silly sod, I would love him anyway. Gosh, Sarah, it's really strange. I've never felt this way about anyone in my life before. I work bloody hard, as you know, and pride myself on being independent, not one of those needy, vulnerable types. But Harry, well, Harry has got under my skin. Being apart from him for the last month or so has been like losing a limb. I've been shocked and surprised by how much I ache for him. When I finally split from Anthony, whom I lived with on and off in London for seven years, it was like a switch inside me that said, 'It's over.' I was ready to move on, but this time, with Harry … *[Bursts into tears]*. Oh, Sarah, how can I make him see that we were meant to be together? I know this is not finished yet. I miss him so much.

Sarah: *[Reaches out a hand of support]* Look, Angelina, you need to be calm and try and distance those raw emotions. I think that you may have to face up to the fact that Harry doesn't feel the same way about you and that he wants to move on in his life. I mean, deep down all men are bastards. You can never really trust them or know what they're thinking.

Angelina: Harry's not a bastard, Sarah. You know him. You've been his friend for a long time; you've known him longer than I have. Do you really think that Harry is a bastard?

Sarah: Maybe Harry isn't a bastard, but he's no angel, I can tell you that for certain.

Angelina: What do you mean by that?

Sarah: Well, he's been seeing some girl called Rachel for a start.

Angelina: Yes, I know about that bitch Rachel. She worked next door to our office. All fluttering eyelashes, such a victim. Harry's a sucker for all that. Rachel is one of Harry's broken-wing projects.

Sarah: I think she's a bit more than that.

Angelina: You think or you know she is more than that? Out with it, Sarah. You have something to tell me. I can sense it. Stop beating about the bush and tell me straight. What do you know about Harry and Rachel?

Sarah: They're sleeping with each other, I know that much, and Harry says that he really likes her.

Angelina: *[shouting]* Well, thank you, Sarah. *[Stands up]* Fucking thank you for that, you heartless bitch. *[Slams hand on table]* I bet it was fun for you listening to me snivelling and twittering on like some love-struck schoolgirl. *[Picks coat from chair back]* Well, fuck you, you fucking bitch. Thank you for breaking that gently to me. I hope you had a good laugh to yourself behind my back, you and your fucking friend Harry and all the rest of your fucking little gaggle.

Angelina throws some money across the table and then upturns a bowl of spaghetti and delivers a parting shot to a concerned diner across the bistro.

And what are you fucking looking at, you nosey bitch? Hope I made lunch fucking entertaining for you.

After the golden rule about how to keep a secret, there comes another lesson – the messenger always gets shot!

In the hours following the incident in the bistro, it was a race by both of them to get in touch with me first. I had been out that afternoon and returned to the house to find the answer machine flashing away. The first message from Sarah was short and clipped, but I could detect the tension in her voice.

"Harry, it's Sarah. Call me."

Angelina's message was equally clipped, but hinted menace.

"It's me. I'm really upset. You need to call me."

Oh, happy day! I thought, sensing catastrophe.

Chapter 15

Enjoy the Silence

First I called Sarah, thinking that she would provide the path of least resistance. The scene in the bistro earlier that day was retold with Sarah adding as an afterthought, "I mean, all I was trying to do was help. Do you think I did the wrong thing?" At no point in the conversation did Sarah question or come close to considering that there was the little matter that she had betrayed my confidence. I felt it wasn't the time to mention it, thinking that she had been through enough already that day. In a way, she had chosen to intervene and she had gotten her fingers burned.

"Honestly, Harry, you should have seen the look on the faces of the other diners. Can you believe that the maître d' had the cheek to ask if I had enjoyed lunch when I left the restaurant? I told him, 'No, actually, I have not! I've just fallen out with a friend who has thrown a bowl of spaghetti all over me and the wine was crap!'"

I wasn't in the mood, though, to console and was already panicking about what my call was going to be like with Angelina. I heard Sarah say, "Look, keep in touch, Harry. At least everything is out in the open now."

So what to do? Call my mate Joe. Joe is at his supportive best and suggests that we reconvene in the local pub for a quick summary of what's happened and to consider the options. Ten minutes later, we are sitting in a bar, scratching our chins and nestling a couple of pints of lager.

"Deny it all," counselled Joe. "There's no evidence to prove that you've been sleeping with Rachel."

"But I told Sarah and she's told Angelina," I argued. "I don't think that Angelina's going to buy that Sarah made a mistake or that she misunderstood. No, I'm going to have to tell Angelina the truth, Joe, and just wait for the fallout."

Joe thought for a moment. He is one of those characters that really do stroke their chins when they're thinking. "Okay, well if that's your line then you should present it to Angelina like it was none of her business who you were sleeping with or having a relationship with. Play it hard, Harry. I mean, do you need permission from Angelina before you embark on another relationship?"

Good line, Joe, I think and make a mental note to use it. Of course I don't need permission from Angelina. "Exactly," I say and we bolster each other up for a few minutes with similarly rousing statements about how independent and dynamic we both are.

"You could always write a letter," suggests Joe.

"That's a good idea," I say. "Apologise for not telling her about Rachel, explain my feelings and perhaps add that condescending line: hope we can still be friends."

"Angelina is confrontational, Harry. Perhaps the letter is a way to calm things down until she has a chance to come to terms with what's happened."

We are agreed then. A letter and it will be sent by email, which she will be able to read first thing in the morning. After a few more pints with Joe, I return to the flat to compose my letter to Angelina. God, why did I not just think of this earlier?

Dear Angelina,

This is a letter that I should have written to you some weeks ago. I hope that you can find it in you to forgive me, but I have lacked the courage, the decency to do the right thing and in my attempts to cause you less pain I have ended up causing you even more heartache.

I gather you have found out about a relationship that I have begun with Rachel and that you learned of this in a most brutal and undignified manner. I will save my full disgust and comments for the perpetrator, our mutual friend Sarah, but want to assure you that I discussed these matters with her believing them to be in confidence.

So the cat is out of the bag and you now know the truth that my relationship with Rachel has progressed further than I have revealed to you. There is no excuse I can give you. I was motivated by a mixture of cowardice and some ill-conceived loyalty to you and the memory of our recent relationship. I thought I could protect you, shelter you one last time. I felt guilty about how swift things had developed with Rachel and did not want you to think that you had been replaced by another after all you had done for me.

Angelina, I think you know that you are irreplaceable. The last couple of months have been a struggle for me. I am trying to learn to stand on my own two feet, but appear to be making a 'horse's paw', as you would say, of things.

Anyway, I will understand if you do not wish to speak to me or have any contact with me for a while. I have acted selfishly and despicably towards you and have no right to expect or even ask for your forgiveness.

I am truly sorry that I have caused you pain and distress. Please know that this was not and never will be my intention.

Yours truly,
Harry

At 8.30 a.m. that morning the phone rings and it's Angelina.

"I got your email," she begins. "I've never needed to be protected or sheltered, not from you, Harry Champion, or anyone. Especially not from you!"

"Stupid line, condescending I know. I got a bit carried away. I'm sorry." This is going to be awkward.

"So, how's Rachel then?" The emphasis on 'how'.

"Listen, Angelina, if you've called for an argument then I'm not in the mood, okay? I'm very sorry about what happened yesterday with Sarah, as I tried to explain in the letter. I knew that if you found out about Rachel you would be upset. I was wrong not to tell you the truth and I accept that. How many times and ways can I say sorry?"

Tears now! "Till you really mean it," she snivels.

"I do really mean it, Angelina. I have nothing to gain by hurting you. Look, I really respect you. You have transformed my life, you have given me so much, but I couldn't go on living with you. It was too hard. So we have to move on and we can either be friends or we can choose to hate each other. I know what my choice is. I guess the other bit is up to you."

"I don't want to hate you, Harry."

Good, this feels like progress.

"I take it everyone knows about Rachel and you? God, I'm a laughing stock. How could you do that to me, Harry?"

"You're not a laughing stock, Angelina. Listen, Rachel and I have been taking things slowly and discreetly. That's the truth. She doesn't want Steve finding out before he goes to Africa and I didn't want you to find out."

"Well, I've found out now." Breakdown.

"Angelina, look, are you all right? Perhaps we would be better discussing things face-to-face?" I hear myself saying that, but can't quite believe I've said it.

"When?" She is sharp as a tack as always.

"Anytime." Well done, Harry. You're an Olympic champion at jumping from the frying pan into the fire.

"Now?"

"Where?"

"How about the service station at Harthill? I can meet you there in an hour."

So a meeting with Angelina is arranged at Harthill service station on the M8, which is the motorway between Edinburgh and Glasgow. Angelina had moved out to live with her parents near Glasgow. The service station is a common meeting place for business folk who have to meet halfway between Edinburgh and Glasgow. I am reasonably happy about how the telephone conversation went. I marked my territory out and Angelina had backed down. I have no idea what to expect at the face-to-face, but will expect the worst and hope for slightly better.

The phone rings again. It's Rachel. She's in a panic.

"Harry, we're in trouble. Steve's found out about us. He's going ballistic and threatening to take your head off."

It just gets better, I think.

"Where are you?"

"I'm at work. Steve had a meeting with George this morning and when he came back into the office he asked to speak to me. He then launched into a fit of temper. George had told him that we were having an affair. Oh, Harry, I have never seen him so mad. I thought he was going to hit me."

"Where's Steve now?" I ask. Should I expect an imminent knock on the door? Steve with an axe in hand perhaps?

George is the managing director of the company that Steve and Rachel work for. I know George vaguely and have been in his company a couple of times. Why on earth would he say such a thing? How would he know?

"What did you tell Steve?" I ask Rachel.

"How do you mean?" She didn't follow me.

"Well, you mentioned that George had told Steve that you were having an affair with me. I would have thought that one of Steve's first questions would be to ascertain from you if there was any truth in the matter."

"I told him that we had been seeing each other, but that we were not having an affair. I told him we were just friends."

My silence provokes further comment.

"Look, his world had just been torn apart, Harry. I couldn't do that to him. He would have been devastated."

There was a bizarre logic to that statement somewhere, but with my nerves jingling and my mind trying to process all this information quickly, it wasn't the time for calm reflection. We had both been slammed into a highly stressful situation and were making the rules as we went along, quite frankly.

"Look, are you okay?" I asked then brought Rachel up to speed with what had been happening on my side: a brief synopsis of the Angelina and Sarah one-act play and my impending meeting, which it now looked like I was going to be late for.

"What are we going to do?" pleads Rachel.

"Look, Rachel darling, leave it to me. I need to go and speak to Angelina right now. At least things are out in the open with her now. I hope that we can sit down and work things out in a calm and reasonable fashion. Let's leave Steve to cool off and I will deal with him later."

I am impressed with my mastery of a difficult situation. I have taken control and devised a plan.

"What will you do later?" asks Rachel.

"I have no idea," I truthfully reply. "But later gives me time to think of something. Stay calm and stick to your story. Hey, do you think this is all worth it? Meg Ryan never seems to have these bloody problems!"

Head spinning, heart pounding, I set off for my meeting with Angelina.

Angelina looks like a wreck. Her eyes and cheeks are puffy and it's obvious that she has had a rough night. I fight a sudden urge to take her in my arms, hold her and tell her everything will work out fine. But I can't do that because I can't promise her that. Not now, perhaps never.

The meeting with Angelina in a service station next to a motorway was calm. Neither of us had slept well the night before and we were both too exhausted to scream and shout at each other. I told Angelina all about Rachel, how we had been seeing each other; yes, we had slept together; no, it wasn't fantastic. I told her about the problems with Steve and how he might be waiting for me with a chainsaw and a healthy supply of bin liners when I got back to the office. It felt good to share my problems with someone. It felt good to be sharing my problems with Angelina. I always felt comfortable with her, apart from when she was stressed and yelling or throwing household furniture items at me.

"So do you think it's serious?" Angelina asked, meaning Rachel and me.

"Who knows, Angelina. It all seems much more difficult than I imagined. I like Rachel a lot, I won't lie to you. But we have never really had time to get to know each other properly. It's all new. We're feeling our way, taking the first steps. Who knows where the dance will take us. There's just so much shit going on around us. I'm tired, exhausted, fed up of darting in and out of shadows, pretending, keeping up the right appearances. I have no idea if I'm the victim of circumstance or if I'm the architect of my own destruction. On a good day I want to beat my chest and tell the world to go fuck itself. On a bad day I want to crawl under the duvet and hide. Sums are not my strong point, as you know, but I think the tally suggests I'm in deficit on good days at the moment."

Angelina smiles and puts her hand over mine. I lean my head in and we sit there together, drinking unbelievably disgusting coffee, our heads touching.

I feel refreshed driving back to Edinburgh. The face-to-face couldn't have gone better. Actually, it was very calm and it felt good to get away from all the madness for a bit. I have no idea what passed between us back there; perhaps a realisation that the relationship in which we had both invested so much time and energy was finally over, a better understanding. Who can tell?

I drove straight to Rachel's office, marched straight in the front door, walked up to where Steve was sitting and loudly and assertively announced, "I understand you want to see me. Well, now is good for me. Meet you outside now."

Actually, the truth is I stopped off about halfway, smoked a pack of cigarettes, worried myself sick about what I was going to do and then had the crazy thought that the best form of defence is attack, which is where the nutty idea to just march into his office and confront him had been hatched. I stood outside the office, lit another cigarette and tried to look hard, dead hard. 'Don't fuck with me, son!' was what I was aiming for.

It worked. A rather sheepish Steve joined me. He raised his hands and said, "Hey look, I don't want to fight you."

For a moment I thought of *West Side Story*, but stifled the urge to click my Cuban heels together and begin to dance across the car park.

"Cool with me," I said, thinking I had got the tempo just right. There was an acceptance that fighting would not be good, but the slightest hint that if fisticuffs did break out I would be ready. On reflection, maybe I just sounded like a prat.

We retired to the local bar and sat down with a pint. A very Scottish way of solving our difficulties, I thought. Man to man over a pint of heavy.

"Rachel called me this morning and told me what George had been saying," I started. "Of course it's all absolute bollocks." I waved my hand to illustrate my dismissal. "Rachel and I are in very similar circumstances at the moment, Steve, and we've been helping each other through, but that's as far as things have gone. We're both just unravelling after a long-term relationship. We both have worries and pressures with business. The last thing we need is to get involved in a relationship." Delivered succinctly with apparent sincerity! So good, in fact, that while I was speaking the words, I reckon I could have taken a lie detector test and passed.

"So where did George get the idea that you two were having an affair?" asked Steve. I could swear I saw his bottom lip tremble. Fuck, I felt really story for the guy now. Of course, I'd known for a long time that it was Rachel's idea to end their marriage. I had witnessed how Steve acted around her and could tell that he was completely and utterly in love with Rachel. He always had been and always would be. Like all men, he had been trying to put a brave face on things, tough it out, act detached, as if he were resigned to the end. I had got the feeling, but now I knew for certain, what his plan was. He would allow Rachel freedom to plan a new life for herself while secretly hoping that, by appearing to be a decent guy, understanding, sensitive, she would suddenly change her mind. Rachel, of course, didn't see his plan and thought he was a decent, understanding and sensitive guy. Steve was all of the above, but he could also add boring and stifling.

"He has no idea, Steve. He just put two and two together and made five. Listen, he knows that Rachel and I have become friends, have been seeing a lot of each other and no doubt made up the rest. In his sad little mind, it's impossible for a man and woman to just be friends. There must be more to it." I let this settle and followed with, "I would like to know where we have been conducting this alleged affair, Steve. After all, Rachel works all day with you and then goes home at night with you."

I could see Steve thinking. I was betting on the fact that he wouldn't mention the few days where he had been away on business, leaving Rachel and me on our own. The times, of course, where we had managed to take our friendship to the next stage and begin our actual affair. I hadn't considered that I was having an affair up until this morning. Up until then, 'affairs' were things that I had read about in magazines. I flirted with the concept for a few seconds, feeling a certain amount of pleasure, to be truthful, picturing myself as the romantic interest, the other man. Anyway, back to reality and my confrontation with a man who was, in fact, the husband of a woman I was having an affair with. It wasn't that glamorous.

"So you're telling me that there's nothing going on between you and Rachel?" finally Steve asked.

"That is exactly what I'm telling you, Steve. Listen, I like Rachel, I care a great deal about her and we have become very close friends. I'm not saying that I don't find Rachel attractive. I can't guarantee you that this will always be the case, that something might develop. All I'm saying is that at the moment there is nothing going on."

"What do you mean something might develop?"

"Well, as I understand it, Rachel and you have separated and have decided to end your marriage, file for a divorce eventually."

Steve nods.

"You're off to Africa at the end of this month. All I'm saying is that perhaps sometime in the future our friendship will develop. I'm trying to be blunt and honest here, Steve. I can't look into the future and tell you what will happen but, as you know, Angelina and I have split up so at some point in the future Rachel and I will be single, unattached and free to pursue a relationship if that's what we both want to do."

Now, if Steve had been a woman I would have been crucified for the last comment. However, I was really pushing it to the knife edge here and had to tread carefully. I hadn't prepared a script before I started chatting to Steve. This had just come out. I was trying to be as honest as I could, damn it, without confessing the whole truth.

"So you're admitting that you fancy my wife, then?"

Ouch! Well, I had walked into that one singing. Actually I had set the traps myself and then forgotten where I placed them.

"What's the right answer here, Steve?" I up the aggression and frustration a wee bit. Again none of this is a plan; it's a reaction. "What do you want me to tell you? I have been accused this morning by your business partner of having an affair with your wife. I have been told that you were hunting me. So here I am, Steve. I came looking for you remember. I thought we could sit down and have a chat, man to man. Of course I find Rachel attractive, she is a bonny woman and you know that yourself, but so will most of the guys in the office block. Is that a crime? Should I tell you a bare-faced lie and say no I don't find Rachel attractive in the slightest; I prefer short, fat, ugly women? Would that reassure you, Steve? Would that make you feel better? Surely, bollocks!"

"No," he conceded. "Look, I care about Rachel. She has been my wife for eight years. I just don't want to see her getting hurt. I'm trying to accept that my marriage is over, that Rachel doesn't love me anymore. But it's bloody difficult, you know. It hurts. How would you feel if the person you are nuts about suddenly started seeing another man, even as a so-called friend? At home it's 'Harry said this' and 'Harry said that.' Blah, blah! The truth is that I have come to fucking despise you, Harry Champion. And do you know why? Because I know Rachel and I can see that sparkle in her eyes when she talks about you. I can see that glow from her when she talks to you, the way she acts around you. All I'm asking, Harry, man to man, is that you take care of her, treat her well." Steve paused as if he were about to add something else but then thought to himself that he had said enough already, dropped his head and looked absolutely gutted, with the emphasis on gutted.

Well, Harry, you clever sod you. You asked for that, you smart so and so, and you deserved it, too. So let's do a quick head count here shall we: adulterer and now selfish bastard! I wanted to reach out and assure Steve that I would look after Rachel, but of course I couldn't do that. I think I grunted, "Yes," but too much had been said already and it was time to move things on. We changed the subject and talked about his contract in Africa, his dreams, his plans. I feigned interest, but just felt shame.

As I walked away from the bar and got in my car to drive home, I reflected that in different circumstances Steve and I could have become very good mates. I understood what he had said and I felt guilty and apprehensive: guilty for putting him in this situation and apprehensive about the responsibility that I had just accepted to take care of Rachel. As a man, Steve had communicated to me, 'Listen, if you are looking for someone to sleep with, a conquest, please choose someone other than the woman I love but now know I can never have. If you really care about Rachel, then you will have my blessing.'

Troubled and exhausted, I returned home, knowing that I would seek solace under my duvet and blissful sleep, or so I hoped.

Chapter 16

Sometimes Love just ain't enough

Today is the first day of the rest of my life; I remembered that oft-quoted, motivational line as the alarm clock slapped me into consciousness the very next morning. *Oh fuck off!* I thought and pulled the duvet over my head again. I wasn't sleeping well and had taken to administering a wee dram for medicinal reasons every night. This helped, but it was becoming a real struggle to get up in the morning, to make it through the day without going back to bed for a nap. Trouble is that after 200 years of Presbyterian culture in my country, going back to bed in the afternoon because you are tired is akin to admitting that you worship the devil. I felt guilty and lazy. I knew that things were slipping away. Some days I didn't care and was happy to raise the white flag and surrender to bed, try to get a couple of hours. Other days were better and I would frantically try to make up for the lost days by working feverishly.

Sometimes I would give up trying to sleep, get up in the middle of the night and just go driving on the deserted roads. I have always found driving in the wee small hours relaxing. I drove north, up the motorway to Perth, one evening and back, a round trip of some 80-odd miles. My only companions on these nocturnal adventures were some old friends on the car CD player. John Martyn or Blue Nile albums I discovered were recorded specifically for driving all alone in the middle of the night and heading nowhere.

After the confession to Angelina and the confrontation with Steve, Rachel and I were forced further underground. We would meet for an occasional coffee during the day and sneak late-night phone calls. Steve, of course, kept an ever-watchful eye on Rachel and trying to arrange a time when we could be alone together proved impossible. We played along and counted down the days till Steve caught his flight to Cape Town.

Angelina and I appeared to comfortably move into our new post-relationship epoch and began daily chats on the phone. In the course of those pleasantries, we arranged to meet at our favourite Thai restaurant. It was an enjoyable evening. The food was divine and the conversation was light, sparkling, thought provoking. She had a good snigger when I told her about my confrontation with Steve. Angelina thought that if Rachel and I wanted to see each other we should just get on with it. How surreal. It felt grown up, though, like we had earned the right to free admission at a *Guardian* reader's relationship convention.

After Angelina and I said our goodbyes, I drove alone to my favourite spot on Arthur's Seat and drifted. I thought about all those romantic poets and writers, artists and musicians who had walked the streets of the city down there, weighed down with their own troubles, concerns, anxieties about love, about life and how it had inspired them to write sonnets, stanzas, songs and suppositions.

My regular access visits with Haley continued throughout this period, every Wednesday night and every second weekend, following the separation document to the letter. Haley had turned into a precocious and confident young lady. I was convinced that she was secretly twenty-five and pretending to be eight years old.

Discussing the mess you had made of your love life with your eight-year-old daughter was one of many idiosyncrasies of living at the fag-end of a century that had begun with people nervous at looking at uncovered table and piano legs. I thought it was only right and proper, though, that I kept Haley up to speed on what her father was up to. Actually trying to explain complex emotional problems at a level an eight-year-old would understand was very cathartic. Actually, as always with children, I have found them to be frighteningly perceptive and we patronise them at our peril.

So, Wednesday nights down at Mickey D's I would provide Haley with regular updates on my increasingly chaotic love life. I had introduced Rachel to Haley and the three of us had spent time together. Angelina and Haley, of course, had built a very strong relationship over the three years that we had all been together and there were a few awkward moments when Haley, in her apparent innocence, would say things like, "Angelina prefers Chanel and L'Oréal and Lancôme when she's choosing makeup."

"Oh really?" Rachel would reply. "Well, I can't afford expensive brands like that."

"Angelina told me it's a false economy wearing cheap makeup and bad for your skin."

To be fair to Rachel, she was enthusiastic about working on her relationship with Haley, but there were tensions there, similar to those existing in the early days with Angelina. It must be hard for any woman to be instantly flung into a situation where there's another woman, albeit an eight-year-old version of one, who is vying for attention and affection from the person they are starting a relationship with. Actually, Hamish helped Haley and Rachel bond quickly. Rachel and Hamish made an instant connection, because Hamish was a floozy, but also because Rachel was one of those women who was just a softy when it came to animals. Hamish saw Haley as one of his herd and watched over her with all the instinctive paternal loyalty that he had been bred for. Haley, playing in the park, would see Hamish moving into shepherding mode, skirting on the fringes, hunkering down on all fours with his head between his front paws, watching, protecting, ready to intercede at the slightest hint of a threat. Haley, having reached eight going on nine, wanted a degree of independence and I had started to let her walk to the local shop at the end of the street on her own. I had no worries about letting her venture out on a solo journey to the shop or down to the local play park as long as Hamish accompanied her. Haley, of course, thought that she was taking Hamish for a walk. But Hamish and I would look knowingly at each other and understand the real truth. Being knocked over by a runaway juggernaut or kidnapped by a pervert was never a concern when Haley ventured out the front door with Hamish in tow. Witnessing Hamish with Haley was like watching one of those CIA agents who are detailed to protect the President of the USA or Special Branch protecting one of the Royal Family. Hamish had been bred to accept that his job was to take the bullet; although, in this case, Hamish didn't look tense or nervous having to chew gum and wear dark sunglasses. Hamish approached his duties with an excited swagger and a swish of his big, bushy tail.

So I had no concerns about continuing my relationship with Rachel and was positive that, should things develop more seriously between us, the three of us could develop a harmonious family unit.

On one of those nights down at Mickey D's I had been chatting to Haley about Rachel. Haley startled me when she asked me straight out, "Do you love Rachel, Dad?"

I paused in shock and said, "I think I do."

Haley looked into my eyes with an expertise beyond her years and said, "The question is: do you love her enough?"

'Did I love Rachel enough?' was a good question. Enough to put up with all the noise surrounding us? Enough to dig in and fight for her? I had been in limbo those previous few months, as always reacting to events on a daily basis. I had been rejecting this pressure of jumping to a conclusion, thinking that somehow I could take, or rather that I deserved, some time off; that as a single guy I could relax, proceed with my relationship with Rachel, but try to keep detached a bit, take things slowly like those agony aunts in newspapers advise, like I had imagined that most single guys went about things. Trouble was, as always, I had been so bloody intense. My wooing of Rachel had begun months, possibly a full year before we actually got together. We hadn't started our relationship as complete strangers like we might have if we had met in a bar. We had started our relationship and we were already close friends. The term 'getting to know each other' was redundant in our case; I knew all about Rachel and she knew all about me. So it was like the relationship I had begun with Angelina all over again. We knew so much about each other, we liked each other and trusted each other, so by the time we had got together in the biblical sense of the term, we skipped a few months of normal courting etiquette and proceeded straight to making a commitment. In Angelina's case, that had involved us living together. In Rachel's case, it would be admitting to the world, our friends and family and most importantly our ex-partners, that we were having a relationship.

It was clear to me that I had been trying to hold Rachel close and then keep my distance at the same time. I had been trying to let go of

Angelina and yet keep her close by my side also. The trouble was, in all honesty, that I had feelings for both of them. I had been hurt and angry with Angelina at the break up, but that had covered up the fact that I still cared deeply for her, that there was still a connection between us. I also cared deeply about Rachel. Could it be possible that I was in love with both of them?

Haley was on the right track when she asked if I loved Rachel enough. Enough to terminate my connection with Angelina? Did Rachel love me enough to terminate her connection with Steve?

Chapter 17

Cat People (Putting out the Fire)

Lewis, one of Angelina's dearest friends, came to visit me. Lewis was gay and his partner was a six-foot-seven, former Russian shotput champion called Sergey. Lewis was visiting Scotland and he planned to spend a couple of days with me and then meet up with Angelina before they both attended a wedding. I was generally flattered that Lewis wanted to maintain a friendship, post-Angelina. The cynic in me, however, thought that he was truly motivated by curiosity and a desire to discover all he could before reporting back to his Angelina. Not for the first time, I was snared by my easy-going, nice persona, which meant I had to invite a potential spy into my midst. No problem, though, I thought. Harry Champion could deal with a little bit of emotional espionage! As it happened, his visit coincided with a trip by Rachel and Steve to relatives in Ireland, so the coast was clear for a couple of days and I thought I could settle down and enjoy the weekend with Lewis.

On his first night of visiting, we spent a pleasant evening at a favourite Indian restaurant. Lewis had been working for the last four years in the former Soviet Union, toggling between Moscow and Azerbaijan, working for an American mining and mineral company. He declared that one of the biggest things he missed about living in the UK was his favourite Indian food and particularly any tandoori dish. Lewis followed his starter of papadums served with chutneys with a whole tandoori chicken and a couple of sides. He also demolished a couple of gigantic naan breads and then washed everything – and I mean everything – down with uncountable litres of Indian Cobra Beer. Lewis, it's fair to say, has a healthy appetite!

Before retiring to bed later that evening, Lewis asked me about Angelina.

"Is it over, then?"

I tried to give him an honest appraisal and explain to him the pressure that I had felt working and living together with her. "I couldn't go on living under that level of intensity. For my sanity's sake I needed a break. Now I don't know what the future holds, Lewis, but guess what? Making no decision about my future is still making a decision. In fact, sometimes making no decision is a really attractive middle ground, rather than being forced to make a choice one way or another. I read somewhere that there are only two important questions in life: whether to stay or whether to let go. At the moment, I have concluded that I am not capable of making the right decision, so I will not make any. My plan, if we must call it that, is simply to have a little peace and maybe get some fun back in my life."

Lewis then asked me about Rachel. I played it all down.

"We're good friends, Lewis, but the last thing I need right now is another relationship."

"Angelina really loves you," Lewis told me. "Listen, I've known her for years and she's had other men before, but with you she was different. All of Angelina's friends agree; we've noticed such a difference in her since she met you."

As I lay in my bed that night, replaying the events and conversations of the day, I noted that I had told Lewis that I didn't need a new relationship with Rachel. Of course I was having a relationship with Rachel, but we were meaning long-term, fully committed here. What I needed to establish, I thought as I tried to drift off into sweet oblivion, was did I want to pursue a fully paid-up, long-term commitment with Rachel so soon after breaking up with Angelina?

Chapter 18

Heartbeats

Somebody French-sounding talked about it being possible to be the master of what you do, but never of what you feel. Not that understanding our feelings is something we do. We act on or repress our impulses and spend most of our lives misunderstanding what our most important thoughts and feelings are. Steve finally left for Africa, which meant that Rachel and I had more time to explore where we might be heading. I would often cook an evening meal for her and she would, more times than not, stay over at my flat. This was a very romantic phase, lots of long walks with Hamish and pillow talk into the wee small hours of the morning.

We were invited to a party and ended up at a nightclub. Even though all her colleagues were there and we were still supposed to be a secret, we ended up on the dancefloor and could hardly keep our hands off each other.

During the days, however, things were not so idyllic. I was running out of money fast. Angelina had paid both of us a small monthly salary and we boosted our incomes, like most small business owners, with an annual dividend and healthy monthly expenses claims. Angelina and Rodger may have made me temporarily responsible for the business, but I had no access to any of the bank accounts or funds, which were still controlled by them. I had been ramping up personal spending on my credit and debit cards and was now heavily in meltdown and overdraft. I know we had been told that we should pull in our belts, but I needed to make a huge 'expenses' claim to clear off some of my debt.

The news from the Swedes was encouraging at least. They had completed their due diligence, they liked what we had achieved and they had instructed their lawyers to make a formal offer. As a condition of the sale, they wanted to maintain all the current staff contracts and offer me the post of creative director for a minimum period of two years. Their vision was to expand through online services and that was where everyone on the planet was heading. We all waited with our fingers crossed to learn just how much that offer would be and my colleagues and I all hoped that the influx of new cash would also result in a pay rise. Quite rightly, the guys felt that they had been willing to accept a smaller salary while the venture was reasonably new and small, but if they were going to be working for an international publishing company then they wanted to be rewarded for all their hard work and commitment.

Although absent from the day-to-day running of the business, Angelina was always available for consultation when I needed clarification or simply a wee chat. Whilst my short-term future, at least at work, looked settled, it wasn't exactly inspiring. I had doubts that I would be able to work as an employee after so many years working freelance or within my own company. Angelina's career, however, seemed to be very much on the ascendancy. She had impressed the 'investment angels' that she was working for and they were beginning to expand her input into more and more of their projects. My expenses claim had triggered a request for a meeting and I met up with Angelina one afternoon.

"Fuck, Harry! What the hell have you been up to?"

I sensed that this question didn't need a response. I had brought along a rather large pile of demands, bank and credit card statements, which I had been doing my best to ignore for the last month or so. These were not company finances, since I was not trusted with those. No, this was my own personal financial doo-doo. Still, it was a form of release or confessional, to finally share the burden, take the mask off, to be discovered. I remember when I was a kid, my younger sister and I had been messing about in the house when my parents had been out and our game got a bit boisterous. I remember falling onto a little antique table that had been some family heirloom and snapping one of the little spindly legs in two. It was a clean break and I managed to put together a fairly decent repair, if I say so myself, with a tub of Airfix glue and some brown boot polish. The leg held and you couldn't see the crack. For the next however many hours, days and weeks, though, every time either one of my parents went near that table my heart would miss a beat. I remember saying my prayers at night, desperately pleading with God to make that Airfix glue hold. Finally, my hastily arranged repair gave up and we were all watching television one night when the leg gave in and folded in on itself.

"How the hell?" I heard my father say as he bent down to examine the damage.

"It was me! I did it!" I confessed. I just couldn't take the strain any longer. I felt a mixture of shame and relief that I no longer had to carry that burden. It was the same feeling of relief I felt now with Angelina running her practised eye over my finances.

"Well, it's a mess, Harry. I just can't believe you. Why have you not said anything before? I mean, what have you been living on?"

"My credit card," I guiltily replied.

"How much have you put on your credit card?" she snapped back.

Pulling the credit card statement from my pocket, I handed it over like a guilty schoolboy and after a few moments, she pronounced, "Well, it's not as bad as I thought it might be."

"Really?" I said.

She turned and gave me a big hug. "You know that you are just completely useless at finances, Harry Champion. What goes on in that head of yours?" she asked, knocking on my head like she was trying to get in.

"Wish I knew. I've lost the instruction manual."

So we had reached rock bottom and this was the public shaming. All you could do was laugh. Harry Champion, nearly forty years old, had spent all of eight weeks on his own trying to be an independent adult and he had crashed and burned.

"You know that I should tell you to go fuck yourself, Harry? I mean now you might understand what I've been trying to tell you for the last three years. It's not easy running a business and juggling all this." She nods towards all the paperwork. "You called me a nag, Harry. Do you see now what I was going through?"

I nodded, thinking, *Just help me, Angelina!*

Angelina did help me. Within two weeks I was back on track again. I was emailed a list of tasks every day from Angelina – phone the Inland Revenue, phone the copier company, pay this cheque here, do this, do that. We were a team again, but it wasn't all rosy.

Angelina reckoned I couldn't afford to live in the flat. I would need to find a lodger or move out to somewhere smaller that I could realistically afford.

Why did I let Angelina help with all of this and where was my pride? It's a perfectly respectable question to ask. The answer is that life is a team game. Angelina is the person I know who is good at that stuff. Why would I not ask for her help?

With Steve in Africa, Rachel began to put the wheels in motion to finalise their separation. The first action was to put their flat on the market. We talked briefly about her moving in as a lodger, but I was less keen than she was. I reckoned that if we were going to build on our relationship, the last thing we needed was to be reliant on each other for a roof over our heads. It felt like repeating the mistakes of the past for me. Rachel had her next year mapped out for her anyway, as the plan was for her to join Steve in Cape Town, where she would work in the company that he had set up over there. So all talk of moving in was premature anyway as she could hardly be expected to pay rent for a flat in Scotland that she wasn't even going to be living in. I decided that I would move out.

"I hate my job and I can't stand that bastard creep George one minute longer."

It was not often that Rachel swore or, in fact, lost her temper, but she came for dinner at the flat one night after work as normal and was in a real fizz.

"What's wrong, Rachel? Sit down; let me make you a cup of tea."

George, her boss, had called everyone in Rachel's company together for a meeting, it transpired, and informed them all that they would have to take a cut in salary. Same old story, a client hadn't paid on time and the bank was nervous about extending overdraft facilities with no personal guarantees.

"But you guys have been working all the hours on this contract," I reasoned.

"Don't I bloody know it? We've worked our tails off delivering this demo."

"But they shouldn't be asking for work to be carried out for them if they know they don't have the money to pay for it." I stated the obvious.

"State the bloody obvious!" returned Rachel.

See, I told you!

"Hey, hold on, Rachel," I returned. "I'm trying to be sympathetic here."

What had that book said about this stuff? *Men are from Mars, Women are from Venus.* I remembered it went something like women need to share their problems, get it all off their chests. They don't want it fixed yet, they want you to listen. Okay then, time for a change of tack, Harry Champion.

"Look, let me make you something to eat, darling, and you can tell me all about it. I'm sorry for interrupting you. Sit down. How about a wee glass of wine? Chill out while I make us some dinner."

As I skipped through to the kitchen I could tell that the Harry Champion share price had just risen a few points. *Thank you, Dr John Gray and Angelina*, I thought.

I let Rachel get her troubles off her chest, although I still couldn't figure out why she was mad at George. I couldn't see how it was his fault that their customer hadn't paid a bill. Still, it was one of those female things, unfathomable to us males. She didn't like George because he had told Steve about our affair and now everything he did was open for criticism. And they say, elephants never forget.

We settled down for the evening and I said, "So tell me, Rachel, what's your dream? Where do you imagine you'll be in, let's say, ten years' time?"

Rachel thought about this and said, "I don't know if I have a dream."

"Okay," I said, warming to this subject. We had profiled a few motivational speakers lately in the magazine and, as research, I had taken to reading and listening to a lot of their stuff.

"I don't really know," she replied.

Once again I marvelled about how fortunate Anthony Robbins and those guys were that they hadn't taken their first steps as motivational gurus here in Scotland. I'm convinced he would have given up and become a plumber if he had started work here!

"Oh, come along, Rachel. You must have shouted something when the teacher went around the class in infant school and asked, 'What do you want to be when you grow up, Rachel?'"

To be honest, I could never think of anything either when the teacher asked this question. Some boys shouted out, 'train driver,' 'soldier,' 'astronaut' or 'marine biologist' (that particular guy was always weird). 'Taller' was my answer. It still is! Well, I wanted to work with animals or become an artist."

Now we're getting somewhere, I thought. I knew that Rachel back in high school had been a very gifted painter. Maybe she was a frustrated artist; she certainly had the talent. I had seen some of her work.

"I never really pursued it, though," she continued. "I left school and got a job, met Steve and got married. That was eight years ago. I've just been happy to plod along since then."

"But you still must have ambitions, Rachel, something that drives you. I mean why would you want to get up every morning if that wasn't the case? You invested your money with Steve in your business. So you must have had ambitions for that?"

"Well, that was Steve's idea really and I suppose I was happy to go along with it, hoped that we could make a success of things. It certainly had an effect on Steve. He's worked so hard over the last two years and I've never seen him so happy."

In a flash of inspiration, I said, "Okay, let's play a game, if that's okay?"

"What kind of game?"

"I'll tell you in a minute," I shouted as I ran to put the kettle on and grab some paper and a pen. "I have a blank sheet of paper here. Now I want you to take the paper and divide the page into three columns."

"What's the game?" Rachel asked again.

"Look, just trust me, okay. This will be fun."

Anthony, you are a lucky, lucky guy to work in California, I thought again.

"Oh, all right, then," Rachel grudgingly agreed.

I was making this up as I went along so had to be careful as I wanted to create the right impression – the impression that I knew what I was doing. I was working on a hunch at the moment.

"I want you to write at the top of each column the following titles. Starting in the left-hand column, write 'Personal Goals'." *Hey,* I thought, *I'm sounding bloody good at this.* "In the middle column write 'Career Goals' and in the last column write 'Financial Goals'. I want to start with personal goals, so I'm going to ask you some questions to get you started. Let's see what we can put together."

Rachel nodded her agreement and we began. Under the heading 'Personal Goals' I proceeded to ask her a series of questions. This wasn't rocket science, so they were simple, everyday questions, for example: Do you ever want to get married again? Do you want to have children? How many children would you like to have? What countries would you like to visit? What hobby would you most like to take up? What new skill would you most like to learn? By the end of the first round we had filled the whole column with personal goals and they were all the property of Rachel. Then we jumped to financial goals because I suspected that Rachel, like me, would have challenges with career goals. Again, the questions followed the same format: What kind of house would you like to live in? Describe the house. How much would a house like that cost? Have a guess. What kind of car would you like to drive? What would that cost? Picking up from the personal goals, I was able to ask some questions such as: What would a return ticket to Australia cost? How much do you think you would need to save in order that you could tour Australia for a couple of months?

By the end of that round, we had a column filled with financial goals and we even had some targets, mostly guesses, but still at least there were some figures there. Physician, heal thyself. I know I was a bloody hypocrite, since I could hardly be teaching anyone about financial prudence, but still I wasn't charging Rachel for this 'session', just regurgitating a lot of stuff I had spent months reading.

I made another cup of tea and then we began on career goals. Now there are not many people I know who will say things like, 'I want to be the chief executive of the company I'm working for by the time I'm forty-five.' Actually, I do know a few friends like that.

Angelina springs to mind. However, I thought it best to tease out this section carefully. What is the aspect of your job at the moment that you most like? What are the aspects that you hate? Are you a team player or do you like working on your own? Basically, I made it up as I went along, trying to get a picture, not of a specific career for Rachel, but more an idea of the kind of things and aspects of working at a job where she thought she was good, where she was confident.

At the end of the exercise, which had taken a good couple of hours, we had completely filled an A4 page with Rachel's goals. Now I was chuffed as hell, as at the start of the evening Rachel had announced that she didn't have any. I have to say, however, she didn't look that impressed or enthused.

"I'm bored now," she announced. "Can we watch some television?"

I was winded, floored, deflated, utterly gobsmacked! I understand it was all a bit wanky, but I thought it had been fun working together. I knew all the things we had written down would all change tomorrow. Christ, like being asked to name your favourite songs or films, your list changes depending on your mood at that moment. Did that matter, though?

I made some excuse about having to take the dog for a walk and left her watching the television. As I walked with Hamish in the late summer evening, I remember chastising myself and thinking what a prat I was. God forbid that someone could think you were not interesting, Harry. Rachel had been through a rough day for God's sake, man! But I also suspected that this was the first surfacing of some bandwidth issues. Like the scale on a radio transmitter, we were fine within a certain range, but maybe we were not a Radio 4 play in the afternoon couple. For the first time, I pondered the possibility that Rachel and I might not have a future together.

Chapter 19

I Hope That I Don't Fall in Love With You

During one of our daily chats by telephone, Angelina announced that she was going on a date.

"Oh right," I said. "That's good. Who's the lucky guy?"

"I met him at an investors' meeting. He's a chef and has been talking to some of the guys about raising finance for a new restaurant venture. We got on very well, exchanged business cards and he called me the other day to invite me for dinner."

"Is he cooking?"

"No, but he wants to take me to a place in Leith; a mate of his does wonders with fish."

"Sounds good. So what's his name, this chef? Is he a famous chef?"

"His name's Morris actually. No, he's not famous yet but he's worked in some top restaurants in London, including Langan's. That's the one owned by Michael Caine."

"So when's the date, then?" I said, trying to sound genuinely delighted for her and enthusiastic.

"Friday night."

Wow, that's a punch to the gut, I thought. Not sure why, but I was reeling after that conversation with Angelina. She was going on a date, with a chef, an ambitious chef who had made prawn cocktail for a famous Hollywood actor. Why could he not have been some boring fund analyst type? What was she doing mixing with creative chefs, for goodness sake? Angelina's news had hit me hard. I couldn't concentrate on work and took the afternoon off. I resisted going back to bed for a nap and Hamish and I went for a long walk instead. I had this big knot in my tummy as I walked and spent the afternoon trying to figure out my feelings. Why did I hurt so much? I was the one after all who wanted to end my relationship with Angelina. I was the one who had declared my love to Rachel. It was the thought of her being with someone else that really hurt. Completely male and irrational, unfair thoughts flooded me, which could be summarised thus: It was okay for me to be getting on with my life, pursuing another relationship, but I was just not happy about Angelina doing that, not so soon after the split with me. It was the thought of her laughing at another's jokes, sharing secrets, intimacies with another man. The thought of that made me feel quite ill. My rational mind tried to push this stuff out of the way, reasoning that Angelina had every right to get on with her life. She was an attractive, intelligent girl after all and she was bound to meet someone else. Perhaps it was just the timing that had stunned me. I would deal with it, get over it and accept it.

By Friday night I was in a fever with worry. What time was this date? Should I call her? My insides did somersaults all evening until around 11.00 p.m. when I could stand it no longer and called her on her mobile. No answer, mobile switched off. I was beside myself with worry. I was tense, completely gaga by this time. Cool, calm and collected had left the building. I pictured them together, laughing, engaging in grownup, intellectual conversation. He would be marvelling at her intellect, her sharpness, staring into those gorgeous dark eyes, feasting on her pretty face. I bet he had ordered some magnificent bottle of wine and plied her with drink. "Listen, if you want to stay at my place tonight and drive home in the morning," he would no doubt be telling her before whisking her off to some stunning designer apartment, bright and light with a view of the sea down in Leith. The bastard! I hated him, loathed him. How dare he muscle in on my Angelina?

My Angelina? What was I thinking? I thought that I loved Rachel. So here it is, Harry Champion, finally you admit to yourself. You are completely and utterly jealous! Quick check; yep, that's what these powerful feelings are, nothing but raw, undiluted, pure, unreserved jealousy!

I spent another hour pacing the floor before retiring to bed and restless, fruitless attempts at sleep. My heart ached. I felt so alone and couldn't shake the conclusion that it was all of my own doing.

What a performance when Angelina called the next morning. "You called my mobile last night?"

"Oh right. Was bored. Just wondered how your date had gone with the lovely chef." The words stuck in my throat.

"Really enjoyed it, thanks." She was giving nothing away.

I hated to, because it was giving far too much away, but I just couldn't help myself. "So will you guys be seeing each other again?"

"We've made plans." Oh, she was onto me and making me suffer.

"Cool." I was saying 'cool' a lot lately. I had picked the phrase up from Haley. Funny how a phrase so out of date could come back into fashion along with long hair, baggy jeans, afghan coats, Indian cotton and Jimmy Hendrix.

So I learned nothing from my telephone conversation with Angelina and had made a complete tit of myself into the bargain. It's all about the balance of power really. Just after the split, because it was my decision, the baton of power had been passed to me. Boy, had I run with that baton for a few months. But now, suddenly, Angelina had stealthily eased back control.

I spent the rest of the weekend with Rachel, who informed me that she had spoken on the telephone to Steve and had told him all about our relationship. She rearranged the dates slightly, but I guess that Steve knew it was coming. Apparently, Steve was pleased for her and just wanted her to be happy. We both pondered for a wee while what a cracking bloke Steve was. Aye right!

I discovered something spooky while out walking with Rachel and Hamish one evening. It was a lovely night and we had decided to walk to the very top of Arthur's Seat and look over the city. She was looking towards me and I noticed something for the first time – her eyes. That is to say that, of course, I had seen her eyes lots of times, but on that occasion it hit me that her eyes were very similar to Angelina's eyes, who interestingly had similar eyes to my first wife, Heather. They all looked very different physically, yet they all had very similar eyes, the same eyes, the colour, the shape was identical. *I must be an eye man*, I thought. How bizarre. There were other things I began to notice, other similarities about the three of them, not glaring obvious things, but small things, because they were all very different personalities. Well, having said that, Rachel and Heather had very similar personalities. Angelina, on the other hand…!

Curious, but you know those little knick-knack ornaments that you collect for your house? Everyone has them I guess. I'm hopeless at arranging stuff like that. It always looks like it has fallen from a great height in an accident if I try to arrange shelves or furniture. But Angelina, Rachel and Heather shared a taste for these kinds of things and the careful way they would arrange them. A shiny stone would be collected when they were out on a walk, for example, and would soon become part of a display. The way a picture frame would be positioned. Bloody cuddly toys; they all still had a collection of cuddly toys from their childhoods: teddy bears, rabbits and assorted monkeys, etc. These would be arranged together, normally on a bedspread or on a chair with precision. They all shared an interest in the arts. Fascinating. I wondered if there might be something in that theory about men being attracted to a type of woman or vice versa.

Meanwhile, back in Gotham City, I was making plans to move out of the flat. I had been offered a room by a couple of good friends who had the fortune to be living and working in the Bahamas for a year. Their oldest teenage daughter was looking after their house while they were away and they were actually relieved that I could move in and keep an eye on the place. The only snag was that they owned two very large Weimaraners who were completely territorial. I had no idea what to do about Hamish, who was still living with me. It was then that Rachel came up with a plan, which she informed me of one evening.

"Harry, I have a fabulous idea."

"Do share," I replied. "I could use something fabulous."

"Well, my sister Heidi and I have been chatting and the lease on her flat is up for renewal. As you know, she's been looking for a transfer at her work to the city centre. Well it's all gone through. I need a place to live here as well and even when I go to Africa I still want to have a base to come back to here in Scotland. So Heidi and I would like to take over renting the flat here. We thought you could either live here with us and share the rent or you can move out, but perhaps Hamish could stay here. Heidi would quite like you to stay as it will be company for her while I'm in Africa."

"Wow! That's fabulous news. Come here and give me a big hug," I told Rachel.

She was grinning like a cat that had discovered a life supply of cream.

"Now, are you sure you want to do this, Rachel? I mean you're not just doing this to help me out?"

"No, Harry. Heidi and I love this place and we could keep Hamish and look after him. It makes sense for all of us."

It was a good idea, if that's what Rachel and her sister wanted to do. Actually, the more I thought about it, it was a bloody excellent idea. Rachel was heading for Cape Town in February of the New Year and that was less than three months away. The idea of sharing the flat with Rachel's sister for a year was not an unpleasant thought. She was a nice person, very attractive. But, no, I mustn't go there. I was in enough trouble with bloody women as it was!

"You may have inadvertently stumbled across a reasonable idea there, young Rachel," I told her, giving her a big squeeze.

And so it came to pass through the fullness of time that Rachel and Heidi moved into the flat and I moved out to live in my friends' back bedroom, sharing with their teenage daughter, Yvonne, her infant son, Nigel, and the two dogs from hell. Why did I not choose to live with Rachel and Heidi? Well, I thought that it would give us some space. After all, moving in together is a big thing. The other deciding factor came with the news that Steve was planning a visit home for Christmas. Liberal as I am, I just couldn't see us all playing happy families in the flat together.

The legal offer to buy the business had still not come through from Sweden and we were informed there had been a few minor hiccups at their end. Our lawyers were still confident, though, that a deal would be made. Business proceeded as normal. Well, as normal as you can get when you're waiting to be taken over by a Swedish publishing company and have no idea what their plans are. I spent my days in the office and evenings in my new room avoiding the devil dogs. They were monsters and clearly thought that they ruled the house. On one occasion, when I had my head inside a large pair of jaws, Yvonne told me, "Don't worry; they're just being friendly."

I discovered that you had to be careful how you approached Yvonne as they were always watching over her. I had innocently tapped her on the shoulder to ask if she wanted a cup of tea one evening and found myself pinned to the ground within seconds with four rows of canine incisors around my throat. Happy days! Still, they seemed to accept me eventually. Discovering that they liked Kentucky Fried Chicken won me lots of brownie points and I was always up for a drag around the local park, which I think they appreciated.

Yvonne and I reached an accommodation. She had been stuck in the house for months with baby Nigel. So, in the evenings, I would volunteer to let her go out and meet her friends while I played babysitter with Nigel and the two desperados. Haley would join us every second weekend. It was all very harmonious.

Things were going very well with Rachel and Heidi, who seemed to be enjoying their new home. Hamish was in his element, now having two women to fuss and fawn over him. Haley liked playing big sister with Nigel on her weekends and the two of them would cuddle up on the sofa and watch WWF. It was not paradise but it was a pleasant enough life.

Chapter 20

Northern Sky

Just when you think you're following a plan, along comes a curveball, the unexpected to knock you on your arse. My curveball came via Angelina. I had learned that I was jealous of her friendship with the high flying, bastard chef, but was trying to rise above my emotional immaturity and wish Angelina all the best with her new life. I had stopped trying to glean details and clues about her love life during our daily telephone conversations and, to be fair, Angelina didn't mention him again. I dreamed that he had been so awful to be with that night – the pretentious twat – that Angelina had seen right through him.

Angelina and I had arranged to meet up for a drink and a bite to eat at one of our regular haunts in Edinburgh. It was late summer and the city was emptying after the frenzy of the festival. Haley had been nagging me about seeing Angelina again and so the three of us met up at a child-friendly Italian place we knew on the shore in Leith. We had a relaxed, pleasant evening together, Haley extremely comfortable in Angelina's company, waxing lyrical, telling her all about the exploits of the two devil dogs. I have to say that Angelina was looking extremely gorgeous that evening. She does scrub up well, I thought, and there's no doubt that she is a very pretty lady. It's sad that when you spend so much time with someone you lose that ability to look across a table or a room and feel your heart leap like the first time. I guess we settle down too quickly and become comfortable and it's only on the odd occasion that you might catch a glimpse of your wife or partner across a room and think, 'Wow!'

After dinner we took a stroll around the redeveloped dock area of Leith with its swanky restaurants and designer developments. We had to cross the road at one point and I witnessed something that almost stopped me in my tracks. As Haley went to cross the road, she brought her hand up naturally and held onto Angelina's hand. It was an instinctive, innocent gesture that touched me enormously. I can't tell you why, but there was something profoundly moving about that little moment. There they were, the two women in my life, and they were just so natural together. I knew then that I had made a terrible mistake. Rachel was not the woman for me – Angelina was. How can I explain that to you? There is no logic to it, so I won't begin. I just knew, that's all. Like, for a split second, God froze the world and there I saw Angelina with Haley, holding onto each other. I saw my future and this was what my new family would look like, this was the new team I should support.

As I drove home from Edinburgh that evening, I wondered how I might unravel the mess, the shambles I had created. Of course I had no indication that Angelina would take me back and no idea how I was going to break the news to Rachel. My heart pounded. Why did I conspire to make my life so complicated?

I spent a reasonably quiet weekend with Haley while I pondered what I was going to do. Sunday evening came around and I dropped Haley back at her mother's. On my way back home, I called in on Rachel. Life would have been so much easier had I walked in and discovered her in *flagrante delicto* with the local cricket team, but instead she was really pleased to see me. Actually, I was clutching at straws. I would have been crushed if I had found Rachel with even the wicket keeper.

"How was your weekend?" she asked.

"It was fine, thanks." Thought it wasn't the best thing to share that Haley and I had met Angelina for dinner.

Rachel had this habit of always looking down at her feet when she was about to ask something awkward or that she was not comfortable with. "Listen, if it's okay, I would like to come along with you guys some weekend. I know that Haley's your daughter and that your time together is precious and I would never wish to come between you, but you know I was just thinking, hoping, that maybe you guys could take me along with you sometime."

"Of course," I said, because, well … because what else was I going to say? And at that moment that's what I wanted to say. For all that had happened inside my head over the last twenty-four hours, I hadn't suddenly stopped having a genuine affection for Rachel.

"Listen, why don't you come along with us on Wednesday night?" I heard myself saying. "It's not much, but I can throw in a Big Mac. Now how can you tell me I'm not an old romantic?"

Maybe I had been rash on Friday night. Rachel and I clearly had something going here. Thank God I hadn't blurted anything out to Angelina.

"I really enjoyed Friday night," opined Angelina first thing Monday morning. "It was really great to see Haley again. You should be very proud of her, Harry. She's a really wonderful, friendly, happy little girl."

"Thank you," I said.

"Listen, I've been thinking. How would you like to spend a weekend away together sometime?"

"What did you have in mind?" I was dreaming, surely.

"Well, I really miss you and, you know, I thought we could make some excuse and disappear for a weekend together."

"What about your chef?" I asked, really meaning, 'What about Rachel?'

"He's a prat. I only went out with him that one time and he spent the evening talking about himself. I got the impression that was his favourite subject and didn't like to interrupt. I laughed more on Friday night and really enjoyed myself. Look, Harry, what's a girl to do to get a dirty weekend with you? Hit you over the head with a club and drag you off?"

"Sorry, I charge extra for that," I replied. "Look, I would love to go away with you, Angelina. I really have missed you and enjoyed Friday night as well. When Haley took your hand to cross the road, well, it was …" Will I never learn to keep my big mouth shut?

"It was what?" Angelina asked.

"It was a beautiful moment. But, look, what about Rachel?"

"Tell her you need to go away on business. I was thinking we could head up north some Friday night and spend some time together until the Sunday. What do you think? Up for a bit of danger, Mr Champion?"

"I'd love that," I said.

89

Talk about role reversal! So now I had signed up to cheat on Rachel with Angelina. Yep, things were looking a lot easier for you, Harry. Well done. Perhaps the United Nations would be interested in your talents. A mere border dispute would be nothing for a man of your talents.

Of course, I needed a cover story. I had received an email, as luck would have it, from an ex-bandmate called Andy who lived near Newcastle. We hadn't seen each other in years and he had invited me down to stay at his place for a weekend and hear his new band. Andy lived in Darlington, so what better cover than telling Rachel I was going down to Darlington for the weekend to catch up with my old mate Andy? A quick call to Andy and my alibi was put in place. Again, this wasn't an all-out lie because I did intend meeting up with Andy at some point for the very reasons stated. I was just being economical with the dates. Bullshit! I had crossed the bridge from frugality with the truth to the quicksand of blatant deception. Still, I couldn't deny there was a certain buzz to it all. Who would have thought? A wee fat bloke like Harry Champion being pursued by two women, two pretty sexy women, at the same time! *Yep,* I thought, *some of us have it and others just dream about it.*

Where were my beliefs and values now? Then again, I have always argued that what you think you stand for is inconsequential until you find yourself tested. I guess we all like to project that we would equip ourselves with heroics if flung into a crisis – a burning building, a high-tension siege, whatever – but we can never really know until we're tested in that situation. I mean, you can have it all upstairs in theory, but who knows until you're faced with a moral dilemma what your reaction would be? I've heard them all; my husband would never look at another woman; I can trust him; my wife is very loyal; she could never hurt me like that. The trouble with beliefs and values is they are not universal and they are subject to change all the time.

Most of us in the West have been brought up to believe and value a monogamous relationship with another partner. It's a high ideal. Even the legal term 'adulterer' sounds evil. Well, it does if you kind of put on a demonic voice when you say it (think *Exorcist*). But consider Mormons. Now, I know that they pester you at the door and all that, but back home in Salt Lake City these people are fine, upstanding citizens who pay their taxes, go to church, care and look out for their children. Their religion has enshrined that monogamy is not a natural state and they believe that it is okay for a man to have more than one wife. He still can't have sex with any of them before he is married, but, nonetheless, who are we to say that he is wrong? There are other beliefs in other cultures across the globe, which we also would find morally repugnant, but the point I'm trying to make is that beliefs and values are subjective. Just because we've been brought up in a Judea/Christian tradition does not give us the right to claim the moral high ground. Maybe you think differently?

One of the things I have found about getting older is realising that a lot of the beliefs and values I have collected and jumbled up inside me are actually squatters. They are not mine. I don't own the title for them. I've just collected them and stored them away in a filing cabinet titled 'Beliefs and Values'. I have come to learn through trial and error that to be the man I want to be, to truly be 'all the man I will ever be' as my dear mother was fond of telling me, I need to jettison some of the baggage I have been carrying and find out what I really believe and what I really value.

I know what you're thinking; all this stuff sounds like belly fluff, but that's the trouble with being a comfortable sofa. Thoughts like these float into my head all the time and I can't help myself.

So I knew that I was doing something wrong by preparing to cheat on Rachel with Angelina. I knew that there can be no moral defence that I could argue here that would win your respect. But I had been tested and I had failed. If you have been tested and have done the right thing, then all power to you! If you think that you would do the right thing but have never been tested, I would counsel, wait till that day comes. As for me, I failed. I was confused (that old nugget), but most of all I was intrigued. I guess every man has a fantasy about sleeping with two women at the same time. Well, this wasn't exactly the fulfilment of that fantasy, but it was a step in the right direction. So I decided to freefall and see where life would take me.

It took me to a Highland hotel on a 'two nights for the price of one' special offer. I had sold my deception to Rachel and headed north to a magnificent country hotel near Oban on the West Coast of Scotland. Angelina and I checked in and, to cement the debauchery, spent the rest of the afternoon with the 'Do Not Disturb' sign hung around the bedroom door handle. That night we joined the other eight guests (small hotel) for a sumptuous meal and retired to the library where a log fire, a wee dram and some sparkling conversation with the other guests awaited us.

In the morning, I popped outside before breakfast, under the cover story of going for a cigarette, and called Rachel.

"Hi, darling. How are you?"

"I'm okay. Missing you loads, though. How's your weekend going?"

"Yeah, really enjoying myself. Andy's built a recording studio in his garage. We've had lots of fun playing around. His band is very good. Went to hear them playing at a club last night. Very polished sound."

"Where are you? It sounds very quiet there."

"Oh, I'm in Andy's back garden. It's very rural here. In fact, it's almost like being in the open countryside." I look up and see the mountains before me and Loch Awe. From the corner of my eye I see Angelina marching out to call on me. "Listen, apparently that's breakfast ready. Will talk to you later. Bye. Love you."

"Okay then. Bye. Love you, too."

"Breakfast is served!" shouts Angelina.

Phew! Just made that within milliseconds. Heart pounding, I went for my breakfast.

"Have you enjoyed the weekend, Harry?" asked Angelina.

"It's been fabulous, darling. I've really enjoyed myself, very relaxing. It's been great to get away from it all." I point at the scenery through the conservatory window where we were eating breakfast and declare, "Look at that; it would be hard not to enjoy all of this."

"So what do you want to do then, Harry? I mean, is this just the start of an affair or are we getting back together?"

"Do you want to get back together, Angelina?"

"Of course I do, you nutcase. I love you so much. Can't you tell?"

"Angelina, I love you. Of course I want to get back together with you. God, if only you knew what I have been going through. Do you know that I was so green with envy, twisted with jealousy, the night you went out on that date with the chef that I nearly got in the car with the idea of tracking you down in the restaurant?"

"Really?" says Angelina. "So if that's the case why didn't you say anything?"

"I wasn't sure how you would react, what you wanted. I thought maybe you'd had enough of me, gone off me forever."

"Harry, I have ached every night since we split up. I have been driving my parents mad with my sobbing."

"God, your parents; what will they think if we announce that we're back together?"

"Don't worry about my parents. Honest, they'll be glad after all they've had to put up with these last few months. My dad will deliver me to your door. I promise."

"Listen, things will need to change, though, Angelina. I can't go back to those arguments and fights. We'll need to find a way of discussing things and not just screaming at each other."

"I know, Harry, but I have really benefited from the anger management course. It's really helped me. It wasn't always my fault, though, the arguments. So we need to help and support each other if we're going to make things work between us."

"That's true. Listen, what am I going to do about Rachel? You're going to have to give me some time to sort it out. I mean I can't just drive home and announce I'm leaving her and going back to you. She'll have a breakdown."

"How much time will you need?"

"How much time have I got?"

"Three weeks."

"Have you prepared a script or something? Why three weeks?"

"It's in the script."

"Angelina, I need some time here. I mean, what happens when we get back together? Where are we going to live? I take it that you don't fancy joining me with my flatmates, the devil dogs?"

"No, that's not high on my list of options. Okay, I hear what you're saying. I'll get to work on that and meanwhile you can deal with Rachel and end your relationship with her. I reckon that we should aim to have everything sorted out by Christmas."

"You've not made a timing plan and a flowchart have you?"

"No, but I will!"

So with that little war council over breakfast, we pledged our futures together. Not the most romantic script perhaps, but the setting was.

Chapter 21

Into My Arms

My challenge was this. I was in love with two women and two women were in love with me. On the one hand, there was Angelina, a woman with whom I had lived and been intensely involved for three years of my life. On the other hand, there was Rachel, a woman with whom I had enjoyed a romance and grown to deeply care for. If I were a long distance lorry driver and Angelina lived in Cornwall and Rachel lived in Aberdeen, I could have quite happily set up a home with each of them and toggled between the two, maybe on a weekly or monthly basis. However, I was not a long distance lorry driver and the chances of persuading either of the ladies involved to move house were a tad unrealistic.

I could have moved to Salt Lake City, become a Mormon and married both of them. That's bigamy – well it's the least I could do, as the old joke goes (although, on reflection, perhaps it's an old joke best told with a Scottish accent).

There was a middle way, I supposed, where I could attempt to somehow keep both of them in my life by declaring neutrality. 'Look,' I might say, 'I love you both and can't decide. Can't we just keep things as they are and I will see both of you? I promise to be faithful to you both.' And when I awoke from the coma …

No, I would have to choose one and leave the other. Which one to choose? How to leave the other? Those were the challenges I thought I should focus on.

"What does your heart tell you?" Can't you just punch people who offer that as a mystical solution to your dilemma? As if you can just say, "Hang on, I'll just check. Mine says 'Made in Korea'."

This was pointless advice, because my heart said different things at different times, depending who I was with. When I was with Angelina I was positive that my heart whispered, 'I love Angelina,' and when I was with Rachel it said, 'I love Rachel.' So a fat lot of use my heart was. Don't you find that hearts are sneaky like that? I mean, why can't they be clear and speak up when they want to tell you something important? Can't they flash up a text box or something, like Microsoft, saying, 'Are you sure you want to delete this relationship?' Why does everything have to be in special heart code, where the information is drip-fed to you, leaving you in a perpetual quest to understand and translate the message?

As far as I could see, the heart score read Angelina 1 Rachel 1. It was in my mind that I would have to decide who to move forward with and I think that I had already decided this – my decision was Angelina.

Why was my decision Angelina and not Rachel? Well, let me try to explain. For many years I have had a little dinner party recital that I have shared with anyone who cared to listen about my thoughts on relationships. I suggest that we need four types of stimulation in our lives: intellectual, emotional, physical and spiritual. I'm a Jungian guy, so I'm insisting that there is a spiritual dimension to our lives. Anyway, being that we are all designed uniquely, it's self-evident that there are vast differences on the values we all put on these areas in our lives. We are ever in flux, so these values will change and shift as we journey through life. I think that maintaining a long-term, fulfilling relationship has a greater chance of success if we share our top priorities in these areas with our partners.

Intellectual stimulation is important to me. Not that I'm a candidate for Mensa, but Angelina is closer to my profile than Rachel. We like to be intellectually stimulated by the people around us, by the challenges at work, by the films we watch and the books we read. We are both open to the opportunities to improve ourselves and develop new skills and understandings of things. We constantly challenge each other in these areas. Emotional stimulation rates second in my list and I think that I am similar to Angelina in this. I need to be told that I am doing the right thing, that I have a contribution to make. A lot of what I can bring to an enterprise is either creative or emotional. I can describe a vision and inspire people to believe in it. I like to think that I am good at making the people around me feel good and believe in themselves. A corporate lawyer would suggest that my value is in 'intellectual property' rather than bricks and mortar or stuff. Therefore, what I bring to the party is sometimes harder to define. That's why I need to be told that I am valued and told that often. Curiously, Angelina is exactly the same, but for different reasons. Angelina is a highly driven and focused person, which means that she expects everyone to share her values and energy in accomplishing things. She gets frustrated when they don't, when things don't work properly, and she is very self-critical. Angelina needs a lot of emotional support and I can provide her with that in spades, but she can appreciate what I bring to the party, so we complement each other very well. The purpose of this wee meandering and attempt at measuring compatibility is not to question who the better person is, in this case Angelina vs Rachel. People are wired differently. I'm stumbling around like everyone else on the subject, merely trying to suggest that, in order to sustain a long-term relationship with someone, it might be a start to try and define what it is that you have in common and what you're looking for in the first place.

So, using my little parlour game, it looked like it was Angelina who was more suitable for me than Rachel. Did this mean that I loved Angelina more than I did Rachel? Well, it would be very simple and more romantic if that were the case. But the truth is that I believe I loved them both at that point. I didn't have a meter to measure how much I loved them; all I could go on was some common sense and make my choice to be with the one I had more things in common with.

All I needed to do then, to move on in my life, was to find a way to tell Rachel that our love affair was over.

Chapter 22

Poison and Wine

Having made my decision, having satisfied myself that I had reached the right conclusion, I decided to sit down with Rachel and tell her right away. We arranged to meet at my flat (sorry, Rachel and her sister's flat) and there I would attempt to explain why I was going back to Angelina. Rachel hadn't been applying for the job of companion to Mr Champion; she had fallen in love. She hadn't planned it, invited it. It had all happened by accident. There was no easy way of sharing that kind of news.

On the night in question, Rachel was as friendly and as bubbly as ever. In fact, she was very tactile as I prepared dinner for her, continually hugging me and kissing me. Not the perfect start for what I was about to deliver.

"So, what did you want to talk to me about?" she said as we put away the dinner dishes.

"I wanted to talk about us, about our relationship actually."

"Oh. Well that's good because I've got some exciting news for you as well."

This is not getting any easier, I thought.

"Okay, well you go first, then," Rachel prodded.

"No, I insist, you go first," I said. "You're clearly bursting to tell me something. My news can wait."

"Well, Mr Champion, are you ready?"

"I'm ready, Rachel. Come on, out with it."

"You'll never guess."

"No," I said, now getting worried.

"I think I'm pregnant. I think I'm having our baby, Mr Champion."

How can I tell you how stunned I was by that news?

"Pregnant? But how can you be sure?"

"I'm not sure, but I think I am. You don't seem very happy."

"Sorry, I'm in shock. So is it official, I mean have you taken a test or anything?"

"No, but I'm late by nearly three weeks and I've never been this late before. I've made an appointment to see the doctor."

"Right, when?"

"Tomorrow. Oh, Harry, it's so exciting, don't you think?" Rachel threw herself around my neck again and snuggled into me.

"Well, listen, Rachel, I don't want to be a party pooper, but you don't know for certain yet. I mean if you are pregnant then that's a big responsibility. But let's wait until we know for sure, okay?"

"I know, I know. Sorry. I've been getting carried away with myself but it's just so exciting. It's just I could never imagine having kids with Steve. But with you, well, I know that you would make a great father. You already are."

"Have you told anyone?" I asked.

"Only my sister and that's why she's made herself scarce tonight. She knows that I was going to tell you the news."

"So what do you think? Come on, Harry, tell me what you're feeling right now."

"Well, I'm sorry, Rachel, but I find it hard to get excited when the news isn't certain. It's like someone saying I think you've won the lottery but I need to check the numbers first. I feel excited about the prospect, but disappointed that it's not a certainty."

"I know, I know, but if I am pregnant, expecting our baby, what will you think?"

"I don't know what to think; my head's spinning at the moment. God, Rachel, do you really think you're pregnant?"

"Yes I do and I can't explain why. I just sort of feel it, Harry. You do love me, Harry?"

"I do love you, Rachel. Let's just wait and see what the doctor says."

So the plot thickens. I ran to Joe's house, deciding that I needed lots of tea and if not exactly sympathy then some brotherly empathy.

Joe and I position ourselves around his little kitchen table as we have done many times and I bring him up to speed with the events of the weekend, first with Angelina and now the bowel-loosening news from Rachel.

"I think that the best thing to do here is to try and keep centred on what you can do at the moment rather than let your mind race ahead to what ifs," summarises Joe. "In fact, there's not a lot you can do until you find out if Rachel really is pregnant."

I know he's right, but I can't stop my brain racing ahead. "But what if she's pregnant, Joe? Bloody hell! What am I going to do?"

"Well, let me ask you a question," says Joe, clearly frustrated that he has been unable to stop my mind racing ahead. "You had spent a lot of time considering what you were going to do before, during and after the weekend. Your decision was that you wanted to get back with Angelina and see if you could build a future with her. If that is the case, if that is really what you wanted to do, how does the news from Rachel change that?" Joe is a master at playing devil's advocate.

"Well, let me try and meet that dilemma head on. I can see where you're going, Joe, and it's a good question. First of all, if Rachel is pregnant, there's a moral issue to be considered. Can I really leave her to go through a pregnancy all on her own while I bugger off with Angelina? The child will be mine as well and I will have responsibilities. Secondly, let us consider what Angelina will think and do. I mean up till now she's been willing to consider getting back together with me because I'm sure she thinks that I've been having a fling with Rachel. If she finds out that Rachel's going to be having my child, something that will bind the two of us together forever, then will she still think that I'm such a good bet for the future? I don't think she will. I think that Angelina will think that it's all just too complicated and she'll tell me to go fuck myself."

"I take it that, if Rachel is pregnant, you believe that she will go ahead and have the baby?" asks Joe.

"I would stake everything I own that Rachel's decision will be to have the baby," I say and feel certain that there is no point in considering any other scenario. I know Rachel. I know how she views children. There's just no way she would even consider getting rid of her child."

"Listen, mate, I can simply return to my previous conclusion, which is that there is nothing you can do, there is nothing to decide until you know for certain that Rachel is pregnant. If she is then you will need to consider all the points that you have highlighted. But if she's not pregnant then, as far as I can see, the decision that you made at the weekend still holds. Unless you're having second thoughts?"

"Joe, I think I'm well past second thoughts, mate. I think we're in double figures by this time."

I went home to my rented bedroom and lay in the dark on my bed, thinking what a fool I had been. How could I have acted so despicably and have messed up two people's lives so much? Not only that, I claimed to love and care about the two of them deeply. *My God, Harry,* I told myself, *I would hate to see the damage you could do if you really thought about it, if this is what you can do by accident.*

A couple of days of sheer hell passed with me in a daze, going through the motions. I was unable to do or say anything as I was paralysed by stress. Rachel went to the doctor, took a pregnancy test and they sent her samples off to the lab. We all waited on the results. She called me a couple of days later.

"I'm not pregnant, Harry. I just got word from the doctor and the test was negative."

She was clearly upset and I tried as much as I could to console her, telling her that it was clearly not meant to be at this moment in time; that we had been fortunate because having a baby together was just not in our plans at the moment; that we would need to be careful in future. I was so relieved, though, in truth. I felt like I had been awarded a last-minute pardon from the governor or the Home Secretary, like a huge weight had been lifted from my shoulders.

Angelina called with the news that she had booked us a holiday in Spain for October.

"I told my parents that we were getting back together, Harry, and they were so delighted. My mother suggested the holiday, Harry, and Dad has given us the money, suggesting that we get away on our own for a wee while and sort things out. I just got on the internet and have managed to get us a decent break in Tenerife for ten days, leaving in three weeks' time."

"That's tremendous, Angelina." I tried to sound enthusiastic.

"So how are things going with Rachel? Have you told her yet?"

"No, Angelina, I haven't told her yet. Rachel got some bad news the other day and she's been very down, very low. I've been waiting for an opportunity to tell her, but I've not found a good time yet."

"There will never be a good time, Harry. You just need to be bold and tell her straight. Unless of course you're having second thoughts?"

I spend the rest of the telephone call with Angelina sobbing, trying to convince her that I am not having second thoughts, and I make a commitment to her that I will tell Rachel soon. Being Angelina, she doesn't let me away with soon and she makes me promise that I will tell Rachel before the week is over.

I had no wish to regurgitate and pore over the conclusions I had reached a few days before. I had accepted my situation, that I really was in love with both Rachel and Angelina, I would really rather not break from either of them, but that was not a choice available to me. I had decided that Angelina was the woman to invest my future in after some considerable internal debate and even though the scary prospect of Rachel expecting a baby had knocked me off track for a few days, there was nothing that had happened to alter my conclusion. Let's face it, there was no way that Rachel was going to like the news that I had to share with her. There was no time in the immediate future or circumstance where she would accept my decision without feeling like I had betrayed her, misled her. I was not going to emerge from the situation that I had created as a hero. So I may as well get it over with, I thought. Perhaps I should have prepared a script, but my plan was to break the news and then take the flack as it came my way. It was going to be a nightmare, so let's just get on with it.

"Rachel, I've got something to tell you. Can you sit down? This is going to take a wee while."

Rachel could tell by my expression that something was wrong. The mood of friendliness, familiarity was over. She slumped into the chair.

"I've decided to go back to Angelina."

Silence. The absolutely worst reaction I could have hoped for.

"Look, there's no gentle way of positioning this. I know you'll want an explanation, but I'm not sure there is one that I can give you.

102

As you know, Angelina and I have still got a lot of things to unravel, financial and business commitments, and we want to get together again and see if we can make a go of things when we don't have the pressures of running a business in the way."

"So, wait a minute, Angelina and you have this all planned, do you? You have been arranging all this behind my back no doubt. So what have I been then, Harry? A fling and ego trip? The younger woman for you to satisfy your ego with before you go back to the wife? I hope you had a good time, then. I hope that I didn't disappoint."

"I think you know that you've been more than that, Rachel."

"Really? well, I only have your word for that. A few days ago you were telling me shit about becoming a father and all the time you were planning to leave me in the lurch and run back into the arms of Angelina. God, what a stupid bitch I've been and here was me thinking that I had finally found a man that was different. But you're just the same, Harry Champion. Just the same as every man that I have ever met who just wants to use me then throw me away when you've had your fill. Did you and Angelina have a good laugh, then? Bet you did."

"No one has been laughing, Rachel. This has been a difficult decision."

"Oh, my heart bleeds for you, poor soul. I must have fucked up your plans when you thought that I was expecting your baby. Oh my God, to think that I sat here the other week feeling all excited, hopeful that we might build a future together. And all that time you were sitting here … That's what you wanted to tell me last week, wasn't it? I remember now; you called me in the afternoon and said you wanted to chat to me. But you never said anything because, of course, like a lunatic, I was so excited by my news you didn't have the heart to tell me. Oh right, well, now it all makes sense. How could you, you bastard? How could you do that to me? Don't you feel any shame?"

"I'm sorry, Rachel."

"You were the first to say that you loved me, remember? You whispered it. 'I love you, Rachel.' You said it, Harry. I didn't force you. You made me hope, Harry. You made me believe and it was all a lie. A big fat fucking lie!"

"Rachel, look, I'm very sorry. Maybe I should just leave."

"Of course. Don't want to keep you, Harry Champion. You have a life to organise, to plan. Unlike me, of course. I've just got pieces to pick up and try and put together."

Rachel really does have the soul of a poet. That's one of the things I loved about her. There was not much more to say to her at this point and I just sat there until she shouted herself into exhaustion. What could I say at a time like this, after I had just ripped her heart out? Let's just be friends? She was right, of course; I had broken every rule. It was me who whispered 'I love you' first, all those months back. Why? Because I had felt it at the time. I'm impulsive like that and now, having said the L-word, I was snared by it. Of course, had I said back then, 'Look, I really care about you, Rachel,' then everything would have been okay now, would it? She would have just said, 'Oh okay. Listen, these things happen,' and wished me well.

I finally left a crumpled and dejected Rachel and returned to my lair feeling like the love rat she had called me.

Chapter 23

In Your Eyes

Angelina made plans for our holiday together with her usual efficiency. She was relieved to hear the news that I had finally told Rachel, although I pointed out that there were elements of unfinished business that I needed to attend to. Hamish, for example, was now happily ensconced with Rachel and her sister. It was clear that I would need to discuss these things with Rachel, but I was reluctant to get in touch given the outcome of our last meeting. I couldn't think of a way I might broach these subjects with Rachel and it seemed heartless to call her up and say, 'Hi, Rachel, can I have my dog back?'

Rachel solved the problem by calling me at work and we arranged to meet for lunch on the shorefront. I saw her sitting on the bench. She was slumped and I could tell that she had been crying. I sat down beside her and even Hamish seemed to scowl at me.

"How are you?"

"I'm okay. Bearing up."

"Good," I said and squeezed her hand. I wasn't sure if that was in the rules or not, but it occurred to me that yesterday this woman and I had been lovers, so how could I pretend that today we were strangers?

"Do you want to shout at me some more?" I asked her.

"No. I'm all shouted out, Harry. Thanks for offering, though."

We both smiled and I put my arm around her and squeezed her in close beside me. As I have said, this was not about suddenly waking up and not liking Rachel. I cared about the person sitting next to me on this park bench very deeply. She was my friend and had become my lover. Mad, I know, since the person who had caused her all the pain in the first place was me. But I don't know; maybe we could get through this and go back to being friends again?

We sat in silence for a while, watching Hamish running around, chasing a stick.

"I really thought that you loved me, Harry," Rachel whispered eventually.

"I do love you, Rachel."

"But I don't understand. If you love me why are you leaving me?"

Simple question really and clearly the thing that was puzzling Rachel the most. I said that I loved her but my actions said that I didn't. It looked like we were together and then suddenly we weren't. What went wrong? We always go searching for clear-cut answers in our lives. It's either black or white, this way or that way, this happened because of that. There must always be a reason why things happen, a correlation between the linear process of events and their conclusion. When we have a dilemma or crisis in our lives, we tend to spend a long time, rather like amateur detectives, trying to piece together clues, desperately hoping for some insight. Of course, when the washing machine is broken or the car engine blows up, there is always a reason. With the help of an instruction manual or the guidance of an expert we can locate what went wrong. But when we try to understand and fathom the complexities of a human heart, try to understand what makes people act or do things the way that they do, why we do things ourselves even, we always run into difficulties.

I wish that I could have downloaded my thought process for Rachel and said to her, 'Here, Rachel, this was my reasoning. Take the data home and once you've recalibrated your limbic system closer to mine, you might have a better insight.'

For some reason, feeling that you are in love or finding yourself attracted and connected to someone is not a secure basis for sustaining a relationship.

"Because life is more complicated than that, Rachel," I told her. "Because I love Angelina, too. My love for her is a different kind of love to the one I feel for you. Angelina and I know each other better. I have a comfortable pair of slippers love with Angelina when with you it's all new and exciting."

If ever I had said something that would come back to haunt me then this was it. Sometimes I wish I would just learn to shut up, you know; if I kept silent occasionally then no one would suspect what a complete tosser I am.

"I have no idea what you're talking about," said Rachel.

And the truth is neither did I, but I knew right then that I had said something that I would be made to regret, because despite Rachel's claim that she did not understand what I was saying, she would remember the comfortable slippers versus new and exciting comparison and that gave her hope – hope that somehow I could be made to reverse the decision I had made. Angelina would in time also find out about that line and would forever feel cheated that in some way my decision to choose her and describe our love as a comfortable pair of slippers meant that I was settling for second best.

For the record, here is what I would like to have said at that moment:

'Rachel, when I told you I loved you, I really did love you. But I do not see love as exclusive. I also told you on various occasions over the last few months that I thought that I had fallen out of love with Angelina, much in the same way that you had claimed to have fallen out of love with Steve. I now know that I do love Angelina. I now know that when I thought that I was going to lose Angelina to a bloody chef that I was beside myself with panic. I now know that all that Angelina and I have been through for the last three years was not a waste of time but an investment in our future together.

'I have been trying to weigh up my feelings for both of you and make some sense of them all. I have concluded thus: that Angelina and I are better suited together than you and I will ever be. Does that mean that I have lied to you or misled you? I don't think so. Why can't you just accept that this is the way that things have turned out and that life is a journey? We travelled along the path a wee bit, had some fun, but now it's time to say goodbye.'

But, no, I didn't say any of that. I was reacting at the moment, on the hoof, as things developed. There was no time to go away and prepare a press release, an official statement. In my explanation to Rachel, I presumed to shelter her, which I now know was arrogant, presumptuous and just plain old stupid.

"Well, I hope we can still be friends," said Rachel. "I couldn't bear to lose that as well as your love."

"Of course we will be friends," I replied and hugged her in close to me.

So, reconciled to my decision, Rachel and I agreed a compromise where we would remain friends. Rachel would retain custody of Hamish and we would maintain our regular meetings for lunch, walks with the dog, friend stuff.

Angelina and I headed for Tenerife and spent most of our time reading and relaxing on the volcanic beach. Despite the gap of three months, there was no awkwardness between us and we settled down almost instantly into being a couple again. We had some very useful and honest exchanges about how we might make our life together more pleasant and how we might avoid the fights and arguments that had erupted in the past and had finally caused us to call time out. Angelina promised to try and control her temper tantrums and I promised to stop saying and doing things that would wind her up, get her agitated, the principle thing being to not keep things from her. We agreed that we would stop putting pressure on each other and discussed the triggers that lit the fuses on the big blow-ups.

I thought about Rachel a lot as I lay on the beach, soaking up the sun. I wondered what she was up to and there was still a little twinge inside, a little flutter just to remind me that my feelings for her were still there. I hoped that they would pass through time.

I noticed that Angelina's way of coping with the trauma we had been through was to reinvent history. I guess that's a popular tool that we all use. It now appeared that we had been on a break, allowing each other some space, but that we hadn't officially broken up. Rachel, if she was mentioned, was referred to as 'that dozy, red-headed bitch' and the impression or illusion began to be constructed of this scheming, manipulative *femme fatale* who had beguiled me with her magic charms, like the snake in *The Jungle Book*, who had carried me away from the light into the darkness. Like a hapless innocent, inexperienced in the ways of the world, I could be forgiven, absolved of responsibility, because I had been powerless to prevent myself. Sisterhood, eh? Of course, Angelina wanted to know details as well and there were lots of questions. What she was like in bed, for example, was a popular one. Angelina had relapses as well where she would become distraught, appalled that I could leave her for another woman and ashamed that she had taken me back after I had made a fool of her in the eyes of our families and friends. How honest are you supposed to be in these situations? I played the whole thing down, trying to swing conversations back to the facts, or the facts as I saw them, and telling Angelina what she wanted to hear. No, the sex with Rachel was nothing special; you are a far better and more considerate lover, Angelina; I didn't leave you for Rachel; remember the sequence of events? Rachel and I got together after we had split up, albeit quickly, but technically, in my eyes, not a violation of the code of conduct, whatever that was. Our friends and family are delighted for us, they were never too keen on Rachel; yes, they all like you better. My best friends think that I have made the right decision.

I don't know why this little merry dance of half-truths and lies goes on, but they go on all the time, not just in relationships; they are a powerful part of the fabric of our daily existence. Perhaps, in this instance, this is how we cope and readjust to our situation. If we keep reinventing our own versions of the truth, then they will eventually become the truth. We all put such stock in telling the truth and yet we accept that sometimes, in certain situations, 'little white lies' are acceptable, unavoidable. So we have a scale and score system attached to lies. Again, interestingly, none of us have actually had any formal training on the subject. We've all just picked it up as we've gone along. So there are great big whoppers at one end of the scale, that include absolute denial, such as, 'It wisnae me,' or inventions, such as, 'You'll never guess who I saw the other day.' On the other end are a myriad white lies, such as, 'I really like your new hairstyle,' or, 'No, honestly, you can't see the spot.'

Angelina and I completed our holiday and returned home. Home. That was one of the most important topics on our agenda. Where was home going to be? We decided that for the time being I would continue to rent my room, sharing with the devil dogs, and Angelina would begin the process of searching for a new flat for us in

Edinburgh. Angelina reckoned that we would have everything set up, ready to move in together, in time for Christmas.

I returned to the office to learn that we had received an official offer from Sweden. That was the good news, but there were manuscripts of conditions apparently and we were all summoned to the boardroom by our lawyers to read through the details as the Swedes required a response within a week. I had more than enough detail to keep me occupied and focused and hopefully out of trouble for a few days and, after all the worries and stresses of the last year, it looked like things were beginning to come together in my life. I began to feel genuinely optimistic about the future.

Chapter 24

Sweet Disposition

Why did I just sleep with Rachel? That's what I tried to figure out as I drove home to my rented gaff and played over in my mind the events of the evening. How bark-at-the-moon crazy was I to have put myself in the situation where once again I was torn between these two women in my life? I had everything sorted out, or so I thought. I had made plans to move back in and take up with Angelina and I had finished with Rachel. So what the hell were you thinking about, Harry Champion?

List of reasons I slept with Rachel:

I'm still attracted to her.

I still have feelings for her.

I'm a weak shell of a man who can't control the bulge in my trousers.

I'm attracted to the danger.

It's an ego trip having two women want me like this.

My head is so far up my own arse.

All of the above.

Rachel called me as I lay on top of my bed with my head spinning around, trying to make sense of the chaos I had unleashed.

"I'm really sorry about what I said before you left, Harry. That was a spiteful, stupid thing to say. It's just that I've been thinking the reason you've gone back to Angelina is that you're frightened of her."

"No, I'm not frightened of Angelina. Don't be fooled by the persona; she's a pussycat really."

"Harry, don't be concerned about what happened earlier. I know that it doesn't change anything. You still intend going back to Angelina I take it?"

"To be honest, Rachel, I don't know what I'm doing. I've just been sitting here going over in my head what happened and the best that I can come up with is that I'm an arsehole."

"I understand what you're going through, really I do. You feel pulled in every direction. You need to decide what the best thing is for you and not what the best thing is for either Angelina or me. Listen, here's what I feel. I'm off to Africa in a couple of months and I'll be gone and out of sight for a year. I don't want to fall out with you. I need you as my friend, my special friend. So if we sleep together sometimes then it will be our secret. You're always quoting that line about us only having one life. This is not a rehearsal. So what the hell? Let's enjoy the next few months we have together. You know when we're eighty and swinging on that rocking chair we may look back at this time and realise that this was our moment. A love affair, like a comet which burst onto the scene and sped by in the blink of an eye. If that's all this is, if that's all we will have, then I would rather make the decision to grab it while I can than spend the rest of my life wondering what if."

"I don't want to take advantage of you, Rachel. I thought that a clean break would the best thing for us. Of course that was before what happened earlier."

"Oh, come off it, Harry. You love all the attention. Think about what I said. I'll leave it with you. Don't slam the door on me yet. I'll speak to you later."

How many telephone calls like that do you receive in a lifetime? A love affair like a comet hurtling across the universe at great speed and then vanishing into eternity? I loved the imagery. I've told you that Rachel has the soul of a poet.

Don't ask me if this feeling's right or wrong. It doesn't have to make much sense. It just has to be this strong, cause when you're in my arms I understand. We don't have a voice. When our hearts make the choice. There's no plan. It's in our hands.

Oh fuck off, Celine Dion, and stop following me around!

It's an appealing line often quoted, 'We only get one life and this one is not a rehearsal.' Of course, little fillips like this are supposed to inspire us all and in this case encourage us to grab hold of our existence and squeeze every last experience out of it. Stop living for tomorrow or for some time in the future when we think we will be able to live the kind of lives that we have all dreamed about. It sounds great and when you first hear sayings like this you would sign the direct debit mandate right there on the spot if you thought it would guarantee that kind of exciting, uncomplicated, 'for the moment' kind of life. But what about responsibility and commitments? Can there ever be a time where you can simply abdicate on the grounds that 'life is not a rehearsal'? I understand that this is not what the motivational gurus are advocating and it's similar to John Lennon's concept in the song *Imagine*, which goes, 'Imagine there's no countries, It isn't hard to do, Nothing to kill or die for, No religion too. Imagine all the people living life in peace.' It's an ideal that floats into our minds and for a few precious seconds we all want to subscribe right before reality punches you in the face. Nothing to kill or die for? I don't think so. So if a mad gunman suddenly burst into the house and grabbed Haley I would just say, "Go ahead, mad gunman. There's nothing to kill or die for." I don't think so, John. But it's a fabulous song for all that.

So could I really just decide that I would enjoy the time I had left with Rachel and forget about the commitments and responsibilities that I had with Angelina? Could I really go, 'Well, I only have one life and this is not a rehearsal, so bugger it, here I go?' Could I really trample over nearly forty years of conditioning, which had taught me not to expect everything in life? The Presbyterian in me was gasping for air.

Chapter 25

Drive

We officially accepted the offer from the Swedish publishing company. In the end, the offer was disappointing in cash terms for Angelina and me. I was installed as creative director and wasn't sure what exactly that role would entail. The Swedes were sending their new managing director and team over to start work that next week and the takeover would be completed for the start of the New Year. I had enough to occupy me then without trying to pore over every nuance of my private life.

Angelina had been busy and had rented a flat for us in Edinburgh. She called me with the details and we planned to move in together in the next three weeks. Rachel was off to Africa in February, so the run in to Christmas was going to be very busy for me anyway.

So my progress report, or rather the press release for the last quarter of that year, ended up being not as bad as it could have been. On a business level, Angelina and I had sold our business to an international publishing company for an undisclosed sum and I now had a fancy job title and a pay rise. On a personal level, I had split with my girlfriend and business partner at the start of the summer and had enjoyed a brief and passionate affair with another woman. As the end of the year approached, I had patched up things with my original girlfriend and was preparing a move and a new life in Edinburgh with her. As I say, that was the press release and on the surface I think we can all agree that I deserved a few congratulations. Unfortunately, in reality, I still had a few challenges to overcome, but I was feeling positive that I could iron out a few of the creases and still complete the full reversal of my fortunes.

Rachel had agreed to adopt Hamish and we had promised each other that we would remain special friends. It was my intention at this point not to take Rachel up on her kind offer of the previous week and continue my affair with her until she flew off to Africa.

She insisted, though, that I give her a commitment that I would attend her birthday party, which was planned for the Saturday evening a couple of weeks after Angelina and I had moved into the flat in Edinburgh. I had no idea how I was going to make this party, what excuse I could give to Angelina, but I agreed anyway, because Rachel was so insistent and I didn't want to disappoint her. As always, I agreed enthusiastically and then thought I would worry about how I could get there later.

I said goodbye to the devil dogs in November and moved into a new flat with Angelina in Edinburgh. Angelina and I settled into living together again, but I would still meet up with Rachel at the office for walks and lunch. Whatever the daily ritual, I would always promise to attend Rachel's up and coming birthday party.

If I ever employ the services of a personal life coach or a therapist, then we shall spend a long time together working out why it is that I spend so much energy thinking that I can please everyone. What is it about me that finds saying no so hard? They say that waiting and forgetting hurts, but, goodness, knowing which decision to take is the most painful. I had analysed and explored as much as I dare and made a decision to get back together with Angelina. Why? Well, first of all I learned that I was in love with Angelina (remember the chef incident?), I respected Angelina, I believed in Angelina and I had faith in Angelina. Our temperaments being what they were did not make things perfect, but I had given up on the illusion of perfection in a relationship a long time ago. On the whole, Angelina and I made a good team, we complemented each other. Angelina stimulated my mind and my emotions like no other human being I had ever met. When I dreamed of the future I found it hard to comprehend my life without Angelina by my side.

Rachel was a very sweet girl and I had connected with that poetic soul of hers and the fragility that came along with that. Perhaps I had jumbled my attraction with an instinct to care for her, but I was no knight and my armour was tatty and of bargain basement quality. There is a mystery around what binds two people together. We form impressions and that's all we have. Rachel had been a summer in my heart, but never the four seasons. I was incomplete, struggling to make sense of the world in between breaths, but I had learned a few moves. I knew that sustaining a relationship required evenness. There has to be equality and nobody ever really changes. I knew that Rachel was not enough for me.

Chapter 26

Paper Airplane

The birthday party was approaching and I was still promising Rachel that I would attend, although I had flagged up that it would be hard for me to sneak away from Angelina. I was told in no uncertain terms, "If you want to be there, you will be there!"

Pulling off something of this nature requires a great deal of careful planning and a bloody good cover story. Angelina had never objected to me having a night out on my own, but she insisted that I give her prior warning so that she could make alternative arrangements. It's a reasonable request and being Angelina she had instigated a kitchen diary where all nights out had to be clearly marked at least seven days before. So I needed to plant the seed with Angelina that there was a possibility that I might be going on a night out well in advance. "I've been invited to a sportsman's dinner," was the seed I chose to plant. I reasoned that a sportsman's dinner offered sufficient camouflage, being that they are largely all-male affairs. Problem is that they are also formal dress, so my challenge here was how to avoid dressing in an evening suit to make real my masquerade. There was always the truth? Nope.

"So, who's going to this dinner?" Angelina asked.

"Well, it was Wee George that invited me," I replied.

Angelina knew that I had a business associate who was in partnership with another George. One was a tall bloke and the other one was short, hence they were christened for all time Wee George and Big George.

"And?"

"Well, obviously the two Georges and some other folks from their business. Builders mostly, a couple of surveyors and Philip and Joe are invited."

"And what's the occasion this time?"

"Oh, they're raising money for Raith Rovers again," I say, shaking my head, affecting the 'Phew! Honestly, I mean it's such an imposition, but you know I feel I need to do my bit' kind of look. Who needs RADA, eh?

"And will you be staying over in Fife?"

"Yes, it's a late finish and there'll be lots of drinking, so I've asked Joe if I can stay at his place."

"I'll think about it," says Angelina.

So the seed was planted. Not exactly a ringing endorsement of my plans but, as I suspected, my tally of brownie points was low and I had anticipated a hard sell. I could have picked up on the 'I'll think about it' line of course. I mean, really, who does she think she is? I am a man, after all, an individual who can choose to do what I like. But if you are married or have a partner you will appreciate that I let that go. It's similar to reading in bed at night. I'm always ordered to put the light out. When I was a wee boy my mother used to do the same and I remember thinking that when I was a man I would be able to read all night if I wanted to. My mother would switch the light out and I would have to dig out my torch if I wanted to continue reading, to finish an exciting chapter. Who would have thought that I'm nearly forty and still using that bloody torch? Well, not the same torch, but you get my meaning. Life is all about compromise after all.

Imagine my surprise when I came home late from work a few days later and sat down to dinner with Angelina, when she told me, "Oh, Wee George called you."

Heart attack! "Oh, was it about Saturday night?"

"Yes, although you've got the dates wrong. It's not next Saturday; it's the week after."

"I don't understand." I really didn't understand. There was no sportsman's dinner and Wee George didn't know about my alternative plans. What the hell was going on here?

"Yes, he said he was calling you about the sportsman's dinner and I told him that you had mentioned it and that you planned to go with Joe and Philip on Saturday. So he said right and that he would call you."

It would appear that by a sheer fluke and the quick thinking of Wee George, my web of deceit remained intact and I had escaped a spectacular unravelling.

"I'll call him later," I say.

Later ...

"Hi, George, what the hell's going on, mate?"

"Ah, young Mr Champion! Good to hear from you. Somebody's been spinning a yarn, then?"

"Bloody hell, mate! That was nearly a disaster."

"It's okay. She mentioned early on about the sportsman's dinner and I put two and two together. I knew you couldn't have made plans to go along with us since I only heard about the thing myself this afternoon. I was calling to really invite you to a sportsman's dinner."

"When is it?"

"A week on Saturday. Look I'll understand if you can't attend. I mean, you have been invited to a lot of them lately." He's laughing.

"No, listen, that'll be okay. I would love to go."

"So where are you really going on Saturday?"

"A long story, mate, which I will tell you about sometime if you buy me lots of drink and promise never to tell another living soul."

What are the chances of that, then? I had managed to receive collaboration that I was indeed going to a sportsman's dinner; only trouble was that Angelina now knew that the date was a week on Saturday and not the Saturday coming up, which was Rachel's birthday party. Not for the first time, I wondered how philanderers managed to arrange their philandering. It was all too complicated for me.

The Saturday of Rachel's birthday party came and went and I, of course, couldn't attend. This was viewed very badly by Rachel and all of her friends. Rachel got drunk, really drunk and had to be carried home unconscious. It was my entire fault apparently. She was drinking because she was upset that I failed to show at her party, it was explained to me. I was inconsiderate and Rachel had been told by several well-meaning friends that she should forget all about me and find someone worthy of her attention. I would have liked to point out that I had been trying to tell Rachel that myself, but there was no point.

119

I managed to look in on her briefly the next day at lunchtime. She was very ill so conversation was at a minimum. However, I gathered from the grunts and groans that my absence had been the catalyst for her binge and that I had ruined the whole night.

"I'm sorry, Rachel. It was just impossible for me to get away," I tried in vain to make her understand, but she was intent on spending the rest of the afternoon feeling sorry for herself, so I left her present by the bedside and said goodbye.

Diplomatic relations were suspended for a week or so after this event. Rachel didn't contact me and I didn't contact her. Another mistake, apparently, I was told by her sister. "You were supposed to call and apologise. Don't you know anything about women?"

"I did call. In person!" I pleaded. "And I was told, if I remember correctly, to go and die."

"She didn't mean that, though. She was upset."

This is an interesting phenomenon about women in relationships. They can say things they don't mean and they expect us to understand that they don't mean them. Oh, and forgive. When we say something out of turn, they say, "How could you say that to me?" Then, when we say, "Look, I'm sorry, I didn't mean that!" you know that twenty years from now you'll be having an argument and they will say, "Remember, you told me …" and proceed to regurgitate something you said in a temper many moons ago, but also the exact moment and circumstance of when you said it.

So I called Rachel and I apologised again and we became chums once more. She invited me for lunch at her flat and when I arrived she had set the bedroom up with lots of candles. So we had a birthday party all of our own and then Rachel said thank you for my thoughtful present. I went on like this all the way to Christmas and into the New Year, pretending to play happy families with Angelina in our new flat and grabbing opportunities to snatch some time with Rachel when I could. I still had as my objective that I wanted to be with Angelina, but I couldn't find it in my heart to make a lasting break with Rachel. It was too hard a decision to make and my feeling was that if I could keep up my little farce until the end of February then the immediate problem would be solved. Rachel would then be in Africa and Angelina and I could get on with our lives in

Edinburgh. A year is a long time and I felt certain that a few thousand miles between us would bring a lot of perspective to the lasting relationship I wanted to have with Rachel. Of course, Angelina knew that I was still in contact with Rachel, but at first she appeared to be willing to accept that the two of us would continue as friends. That didn't last, however, and she was soon applying pressure on me to terminate my relationship with Rachel completely. So I made more promises that I couldn't keep and dug a bigger hole for myself to fall into.

Angelina and I spent Christmas with her parents and Rachel spent Christmas with her parents. When I could, I would call Rachel on her mobile phone. I think that I even managed an hour with her between Christmas and New Year. I guess holidays are never a happy time for mistresses.

The New Year started and I was optimistic that I could see things through for another eight weeks until Rachel went to Africa. Our new Swedish owners had taken over by then and I was working with the new managing director and the team to relaunch the magazine online and a host of other internet services that we were now introducing.

I came home one evening to find Angelina going through my mobile phone statements. The phone bill was paid for by work, so I had no reason to suspect that the itemised billing would be a problem. I was so wrong.

"You spend a lot of time talking on the phone to Rachel?"

"Not that I know of."

"Well, let's just look at this shall we?" Angelina had already analysed the call statement and I noticed that all the calls to Rachel's number were highlighted with a magic marker pen.

"Look, Angelina, I'm not really in the mood for this at the moment. I've had a really hard day at work. It's really stressful working for a boss again and the last thing I need is an argument with you. Yes, I speak to Rachel on the phone. Is that a crime?"

"Well, twice on Christmas day, three times on Boxing day, every day between Christmas and New Year and two times on New Year's Day. Since we moved into the flat in November there's not been a day when you haven't called her on that bloody mobile."

Shit! Could that be right? It must be. There was little point in arguing with Angelina and her magic marker.

"She has a lot of problems." I really should have just been quiet because that was just an open invitation.

"My heart bleeds for the stupid little bitch. I have problems, too, Harry, and the biggest problem I have is that I don't want you contacting her again. Do you understand me? You made your choice and told me that you loved me. Now tell that vile little victim with her fluttering eyelids to leave us alone and let us get on with our lives. It's not acceptable, Harry. I will not be made a fool of again. You either tell her to go fuck herself or you pack your bags this minute and get out of here. Your choice. What's it to be?"

"Look, its complicated, okay. I've no wish to make a fool of you, Angelina. It's just complicated. She's off to Africa in a few weeks anyway."

"I don't care. I want her to know that it's me you love. I know what's going on. She thinks that you still love her and that you're going to leave me and go back to her. I'm a woman, Harry, and I know what that scheming bitch is up to. I want you to end it now. I need you to end it now. It's taken a lot for me to forgive you, Harry. Now you've pushed me too far. I already feel like an idiot for taking you back after what you did to me. I need to have my self-respect, Harry, and I cannot accept this. These bloody phone calls every minute. So end it, Harry! End it now!" She holds the telephone up and waves it in my face.

"It's not a competition, Angelina, you know? It's not like you get a trophy that you can keep on the top of the television. It's people's lives that we're dealing with here and it's complicated. I will end it with Rachel, but I will do it in my own way and in my own time. If that's not good enough for you then I will go and pack my bags now."

"And just what is your way, Harry? Calling her three times a day? It hardly sends out the message that you've ended it with her."

"I'm here aren't I? I think Rachel's got the message, Angelina. Don't you think that she wishes I were with her tonight? But I'm with you because I love you. I understand what you're saying. The phone call thing has been stupid. I've been trying to keep everybody happy. I'm sorry. I've fucked up. But please don't shout and demand things of me. My plan has been to keep things friendly till she gets on that plane. How do you tell someone that's loved you that you don't want to ever see them again?"

"'I don't ever want to see you again. Stay away from me, bitch!'"

"I can't say that. What can I say?"

"I know what you're doing, Harry. You're trying to make this my problem. Well you can fuck right off, you manipulating bastard. It's your problem. I don't give a fuck how you tell her. I'm only interested in the fact that you tell her. Have a fucking friend tell her, take an advert out in the paper, throw a brick threw her window with a message attached. I don't care. Got that? Just end it or fuck off out of here!"

At that she rushes past me and into the bedroom, slamming the door with one of her special Olympic door-slamming manoeuvres. For someone who was surrounded by women who loved him, I had never felt lonelier.

Chapter 27

Goodbye

Rachel was busy making plans for her trip to Africa. I made an attempt at sitting down with her and trying to explain what was happening with Angelina and the ultimatum she had made.

"Angelina's discovered how many times I've been calling you, Rachel, and she's really pissed. So we're going to have to cool things off a bit."

"What do you mean 'cool things off'? I'm leaving in a few weeks and will be on the other side of the world. I'm sure that will be cool enough for her!"

"Look, all I'm saying is that this is difficult for me. I can't win here, trying to make sure that I keep you both happy."

"Oh poor you! I'm sure it's a real struggle having two women fighting over you. Look, Angelina won. You can tell her that from me. She's got you and I'm left with nothing. No, not nothing, because at least I have Hamish, so she didn't get everything. All I want is to spend a few days with you to say goodbye. You can promise me that, can't you?"

That's when I had this wonderful idea. Peter, our new leader at work, wanted me to visit Gothenburg in Sweden for a week and see at first-hand how the enterprise magazine operated across Scandinavia. I would take Rachel to Gothenburg with me. A last week together, the travel, the stay over in the hotel, a perfect solution and a fabulous romantic way to end it, to say goodbye and finally terminate the bond between us.

Later, back in Edinburgh, my scheming quickly began to disintegrate.

"You are a wanker, Harry Champion, a complete and utter tosser," Angelina volleys. "I can't see why suggesting that I come to Gothenburg with you is such a problem."

"I've told you, Angelina. I'm there to do business. It's not a jolly after all."

"I just thought that we could spend some time together. I have a couple of days' holiday and I would love to meet the people that bought our business. I'm sure that I'm capable of offering a few good insights myself. I'm sorry that the suggestion of a bit of romance has made you grumpy."

"Look, I really appreciate your offer of support. Let me think about it and I'll get back to you, okay?"

"You're still a wanker!"

Maybe there's a book somewhere that I could buy. *Infidelity for Dummies,* perhaps? I don't know how I do it. Then again, I was always hopeless at that game, Snakes and Ladders. I always seemed to land on the snake squares and spend my entire time going back instead of forward.

Rachel, of course, was packing her suitcase for the trip to Gothenburg as this conversation with Angelina unfolded. My heart was pounding with panic and I had no idea how and if I could summon up the wherewithal to get myself out of this one. How about separate rooms? Rachel could travel to Gothenburg on her own and we could liaise secretly for a week. There will be lots of meetings I would have to attend and then I could sneak off and visit Rachel. I was being absurd! How big was this hotel? What were the chances of me pulling that off without having a coronary? Think, Harry, think! I could call Rachel and tell her that the Gothenburg trip had been cancelled. Maybe then I could quickly arrange another trip somewhere for a couple of days, just the two of us. She would be disappointed but excited if I actually got my act together and booked everything up before I called her. That would be a better idea; then I could suggest that it would be more intimate anyway, because there would be no business in the way. I was onto something.

"Listen, Angelina, I've been thinking. I'm sorry I've been grumpy about your offer. It's just the stress just now. Look, it would be great if you could come with me to Sweden. I could really use your insight."

"Are you sure?"

"Of course I am. Listen, I'll book everything up tomorrow from the office."

Next morning, I was in the office very early, much to the surprise of my colleagues at the magazine. By 10.00 a.m., I had booked a hotel for Rachel and me in Perthshire – a romantic little place looking over the River Tay set in 5 acres of beautiful Perthshire countryside and boasting its own leisure facilities. That's what their website said anyway. It sounded much nicer than a European Travelodge beside Gothenburg Airport. I also arranged flights for Angelina. All I needed to do was call Rachel and tell her about the change of plans and then call Angelina to let her know that everything was booked up. Also, I would inform Angelina that Andy had invited me to Darlington again for the weekend. It was a good cover and had worked before when I was cheating on Rachel with Angelina. No problem, I thought, in it working the other way around. Maybe I could write *Infidelity for Dummies*.

I called Angelina and discovered that her schedule had changed and that she could no longer make the trip to Sweden.

"Bloody hell, Angelina! I've just booked a flight for you. When did you discover that you couldn't go?"

"About five minutes ago. Look, I'm sorry, darling, but something's come up and I just won't be able to spare a week in Gothenburg. I'm sorry, but you didn't really want me to go anyway. Why don't we book a weekend away somewhere?"

"That would be nice. Leave it to me. I'll see what I can organise."

And then …

"Hi, Rachel, just calling to finalise the arrangements for tomorrow."

Followed by …

"Hi, Angelina, how do you fancy a weekend in a hotel in Perthshire set in five acres of romantic, tranquil countryside with its own leisure facilities?"

"Sounds great. When?"

"This weekend?"

"But I thought you were going down to see Andy this weekend."

"Agh, he's just called me back. Something's come up and he's rearranging."

"Fab! Why this weekend?"

"Because that's when I've booked it for."

"Wonderful, darling. I love you."

"I love you, too."

'The seat of my pants' and 'the skin of my teeth' are phrases that I look freshly upon.

Gothenburg was fantastic and Sweden is a truly stunning country, although a bit cold in January.

"It looks like Perthshire without hills," remarked Rachel.

The people are very friendly, too. Alas, it was all over very quickly and in the blink of an eye I was waving goodbye to Rachel at the terminal in Edinburgh Airport. She was crying as my taxi pulled away. That was it then. That was goodbye. Oh, we had planned to meet before she actually headed for her new life in Africa, but that would be the last time that we ever spent any time together. From now on it would be back to the scraps we could snatch or borrow. Still, as I reminded myself, no point in complaining. After all, that was the choice I had made.

I spent the weekend with Angelina at the hotel in Perthshire and it lived up to expectations. Wonderful food and wine, a stunning location and excellent facilities. Though the weekend was pleasant enough, I spent long moments with an ache inside thinking about Rachel, wondering what she was doing, what she was thinking.

Chapter 28

The One That Got Away

Rachel had one week left in the country. Her plane was set to take her on the Saturday morning. We had five days. I went to see her on the Monday night after work and she was packing her things, unpacking her things, checking her things and crying a lot.

"Is this really what you want, Harry? Is this all we will ever have, a few memories, one summer?"

"Don't, Rachel," I said. "Look, let's not go over it again. You'll only upset yourself."

"I am upset, though, Harry. I ache inside. I just can't believe that it's all over. Nothing to hope for. Nothing to come back to. I can't believe that I'm still feeling this way. I mean, you've told me your decision. I thought I had accepted it, but I'm just overcome with pain. My insides feel like they are twisting and churning. I can't breathe. This hurts so much. How can I feel so madly and deeply for you and you can just walk away from it?"

She was sobbing uncontrollably. I mean great torrents of sorrow convulsed her and she flopped like a ragdoll onto her bed and curled up into a ball weeping. I noticed that the handkerchief she has scrunched into her fist was sodden. I have never seen so many tears. Finally, her sister came through and took her in her arms.

"She's been like this for weeks. I hope you're happy." She waved me away with her hand. "Just go, Harry. You're only making it worse."

What a jolly drive I had back to my flat and Angelina.

When I arrived at the house, Angelina was on the phone. I dropped my briefcase in a heap and moved towards the kettle. I looked around, wondering who Angelina was on the phone to and then I caught her eyes. They were blazing. *Not good*, I was thinking when I heard Angelina say some words that made me drop the cup I was holding.

"Well, that is very interesting, Rachel."

Had Angelina just said 'Rachel'? No, I must have been imagining things.

"You don't need to tell me why you love him, Rachel. I understand that, remember? I know all those things about him and that's why I fell in love with him over three years ago."

Rachel was speaking to Angelina. But how? Why? What on earth was going on? My mind raced. This just couldn't be happening. It was happening, however, right before my very eyes. Shit! Fuck! Bastard! What the fuck am I going to do? I shuddered.

Gothenburg! I heard the name Gothenburg! Well I was sunk then, that's it. It was all over bar the shouting. *Pack your bags, Harry Champion. You're leaving,* I thought. Actually, not a bad idea. I was coming to my senses and quickly moved myself through to the bedroom, grabbed a bag and started throwing some clothes into it. Maybe I could just get out quickly. As I came out of the bedroom with my bag, however, Angelina was standing in front of me.

"Well, that, as you have clearly gathered, was the lovely Rachel, your lover darling, on the telephone. Wanted to get some things straight with me."

"I guessed that."

She was calm, but I was very concerned.

"Leaving are we?"

"Well, I presumed," I stuttered, "under the circumstances."

"Oh, you've been caught and now you're running away. Can't bear to face me, eh? You lying little turd! You weaselling, fuck-faced cunt!" There was that staccato rhythm again – dum-dum, dum-dum, dum! "Well of course it's my own entire fault. You're a liar; you have always been incapable of telling the truth. I guess I had it coming to me. How was Sweden by the way? No wonder you were so reluctant to let me go with you. I bet I completely ruined your little love trip. And what was the weekend you booked? Oh, let me guess, that was the trip that you quickly booked to placate her when you rearranged your plans. All that made-up shite about going to see Andy … That was all a fabrication as well I guess. Well, was it or are we incapable of telling anything approaching the truth?"

"Yes, Angelina. Congratulations, you've got everything right, bang on."

"Oh, I'm sorry. Have I upset you?"

"Look, Angelina, can we just cut the fucking masterclass in melodramatics? I take it you want me to leave? I've packed a bag so I'll just get going. I know that this has all come as a shock to you. I'll call you in a few days and we can discuss it if you like. But I think we've all been through enough today."

Angelina starts to cry. She grabs for some tissues and again I'm startled by the amount of tears she is capable of producing. So, congratulations, Harry Champion, now you have a full house! What do I do now? Just walk out and leave her like that?

"Why, Harry? Why have you done this to me?" she manages to squeeze out. "Don't leave me," she squirms and a fresh bout of sobbing convulses her. She holds her chest and lets loose a wild, uncontrollable scream. This sounds like she is being murdered. The scream is followed by more tears, more sobbing.

"Can I get you a drink of something?" I ask.

She nods and I bring a couple of glasses of brandy back from the kitchen. I hand her the glass and she downs it in one. "I'll bring the bottle," I suggest.

So we sit there and we drink brandy and slowly she calms down enough to talk to me. I try explaining to her what I had been up to. She asks me lots of questions and I tell her everything. I tell her all about my fucked-up plan to see things through to the weekend and how Rachel's flight to Africa would mean we could live happily ever after. I know it sounds like complete garbage, but I tell her it all anyway, about the doubts that I have had, about what I feel for Rachel and how I sometimes wish that I could just see both of them or that we could all live together. I tell her how and why I made the decision to stay with her and how I explained my decision to Rachel and the thoughts behind the trip to Gothenburg. When I'm finished telling her it all, good and bad, the unbridled truth for once, I rise and prepare to leave.

"Where are you going?" she asks.

"I'm leaving."

"Sit down! I don't want you to leave."

"You don't?"

"No I don't. I love you, Harry Champion. God knows why I love you, but I can't live without you. Come here. I need a big hug."

So I get up and go and give her a big hug.

"Promise me that this is the end then, Harry. No more visits and plans behind my back. If we're going to have a life together then it must be complete honesty from now on."

"I promise, Angelina. Let's be honest, I'm just not cut out for this infidelity lark. I'm totally useless at it."

"You're a terrible liar, Harry. You're simply hopeless at it."

So, there you have it, how to go from exposure to forgiveness in three to four hours. Seven steps to follow. And if anyone has any idea how to fathom women, can you please record your theories in a book and I promise that my friends and I will quickly run out and buy it immediately.

I have no idea what Rachel had been trying to achieve with her phone call to Angelina. Hell hath no fury, I guess. To be honest, though, there was something cathartic about having been discovered. I had felt under so much pressure for months and I had been rushing around like the proverbial blue-arsed fly, shuttling between the both of them and hurtling from crisis to crisis. Now my deceptions were out in the open I had the opportunity to wipe the slate clean and start again. I had behaved despicably, but I will plead that my heart was in the right place and I did not deliberately set out to hurt anyone. Circumstances had just spiralled out of control and I had made a series of bad choices. But there was no escaping that this episode had resulted in me inflicting emotional trauma on two women that I claimed to love. That would be something I would have to live with for the rest of my life.

In the days that followed, I didn't attempt to contact Rachel. In truth, I was angry at her for calling Angelina. I didn't understand the rationale for doing something like that and I was also a little frightened of her. Her strategy, if indeed it was a strategy, had been high risk to say the least. It felt desperate to me and that implied someone who was not in control. I was scared what she might want to do to me.

The office was bombarded with phone calls from Rachel, as was my mobile. I refused to answer. On Wednesday evening, I was getting ready to leave the office when one of my colleagues handed me an envelope and told me that it had been handed in to reception. I knew right away who it was from. On the envelope it simply said, 'Harry Champion.' Inside was a letter for me from Rachel.

Dear Harry,

I've been trying to contact you since Monday and it's obvious that you don't wish to speak to me. I only have a few days left in this country and the last thing I want to do is leave with so many things left unsaid between us.

There is so much I wanted to say to you, Harry, things I wanted to tell you, but you have denied me the option of telling you them to your face, so all I can do is try and record them in this letter. I am not very good at expressing myself on paper; however, as this may be my last chance of communication, I will attempt to tell you how I feel.

I don't know if you have ever seen the movie City of Angels, *which is a story of love between an angel played by Nicolas Cage and a woman played by Meg Ryan. As they fall deeper and deeper in love with each other, Nicolas Cage decides to sacrifice his immortality and become human so that he can spend an earthly human life with Meg Ryan's character. They spend one night together and the very next morning Meg Ryan is killed. At the end of the movie, an angel friend of Nicolas Cage comforts him and asks the question, "If you had known that you would only have one night together would you still have made the choice to give up all that you had?" Nicolas Cage replies, "Yes, because to have one night together with a woman I loved, to be able to see her lying next to me, to have touched her hair and skin, to have heard her breath as she slept, was worth exchanging a thousand millenniums of immortality for!"*

That's what I feel for you, Harry. I think you are my angel, the person that was put on earth for me and I found you. I just feel that you are confused and distracted at the moment, but I know that one day you will come to see that you and I, Harry Champion, are supposed to be together.

How can I ever forget what has passed between us, Harry, those powerful feelings that we shared? I know in my soul that you feel the same way.

So I will not give up hoping and praying for you, Harry. A year is a long time, but if I am right then I know the bond between us can never be broken. So I will wait for you. It may take a year, ten years, but I will wait for you and one day I know that we will be together again.

My flight leaves from Edinburgh Airport this Saturday at 12.30 p.m. and I want you to do something for me. I have one last wish, a request of you, and I hope and pray that you will grant my wish. Please come and say goodbye at the airport. Please come and give me one last hug before I leave.

I will wait for you, Harry.

Love always

Rachel

xx

I read the letter and reread the letter and thought that actually, despite her fears, Rachel was pretty bloody good at expressing herself on paper. I didn't share the contents of Rachel's letter with Angelina. I know that keeping secrets had got me in a whole load of trouble recently, but on this occasion I thought this was a secret that deserved to remain a secret.

So Saturday finally arrived. As it happened I had to drive to Fife on my way to pick up Haley for the weekend. I knew that the drive would take me past the airport. I reached the outskirts of the city and knew that I would be approaching the turn off in the next few minutes. The time was 12.00 p.m. I still had enough time.

Bloody Canadian warbler Celine Dion was singing on the car radio, 'Love doesn't think twice. It can come all at once. Or whisper from a distance.'

I parked up in a layby, watching the steady shuttle of planes taking off from the runway. I remembered Rachel's closing lines of the love sonnet she had sent me:

My flight leaves from Edinburgh Airport this Saturday at 12.30 p.m. and I want you to do something for me. I have one last wish, a request of you, and I hope and pray that you will grant my wish. Please come and say goodbye at the airport. Please come and give me one last hug before I leave.

It was such a romantic notion. I could still make it, rush in there, running across the departure lounge. Spotting the back of her hair, her family gathered around her. "Rachel!" I would shout and then we would run towards each other and embrace. Just like the movies. But life isn't like the movies and I'm not Nick Cage and Rachel isn't Meg Ryan. I'm not an angel, nice though the thought is. I don't come close. I don't believe that Rachel and I getting together was part of some elaborate, divine plan. I don't believe that we were meant to be together. We had had our moment and now it was time to move on.

'Love doesn't ask why. It speaks from the heart and never explains.' It's a wonderful sentiment, Celine, and at that very moment in time it was something I really wished I could have believed in. It would have made a wonderful ending to this scribe!

But love is not an omnipotent force that magically brings strangers together forever. It's a fairy tale, Celine, and the tragedy is that it is such a powerful myth that nearly all of us want it to be true and are forever doomed to disappointment because we can never find it. You can't chain something like a heart, which is capable of timeless passion, belief and unlimited creativity, to such a narrow view. Our hearts are capable of loving many times, of experiencing great depths of passion, of devotion for many people. Love is a choice, an act of your will. And the choice I have made is to love Angelina. My God, I know that we have our challenges and we may spend the rest of our lives trying to figure out a way to be together, but Angelina makes me feel complete. Angelina makes me feel secure. I love Angelina and I need Angelina.

So I will say my final goodbye to you, Rachel. I will always remember you. We were meant to be together, but only for a season and our time has come and gone so quickly. We have been privileged, Rachel, because some people can live a whole lifetime without experiencing what we had together. I was never your angel; that was a case of mistaken identity. I did love you, but I could never

134

love you enough. I could never live up to your high expectations and I know that through time you will look back and you will feel the same way too and be consoled with what we had instead of what we might have been. We created an adventure, a memory and, if we are blessed enough to live till we are old and grey, that's something that can never be taken from us. Goodbye, Rachel. I will say a prayer for you.

I drove away at 12.35 p.m. I watched a plane take off. I don't know if it could have been her plane. I hoped it was. I headed off to get on with the rest of my life – my life with Angelina and Haley.

The End

The Trouble with Harry Champion – Playlist & Notes

I like to listen to music at the end of a hard week. I'll start by reviewing tracks that I have captured on my travels with the phone app Shazam and then challenge myself to develop a playlist, which I then post onto my Facebook page. My journeys through online music sites and reviews take me to all sorts of nooks and crannies. It was during one of these Friday sessions that I had the idea to make the chapter titles in the Harry Champion novel a parallel playlist (but not in an Alan Partridge way). After many enjoyable hours of listening and enzyme-altering litres of gin, I settled upon the following:

Listen to the Harry Champion Soundtrack on Apple Music.
https://itunes.apple.com/gb/playlist/harry-champion-soundtrack/idpl.a63779b9866a444d8f36deaffb3f79aa

1. Spoons - Rudimental (feat. MNEK & Syron)
'I think I'm about to fall' – good lines to begin Harry's adventure.

2. Everybody Knows - Leonard Cohen
Smoky, late-night lyrics growled by LC. A masterclass in effortless lyric application and manipulation.

3. There's a Place in the World for a Gambler - Dan Fogelberg
There's a song in the heart of a woman that only the truest of loves can release.

4. Waiting for My Real Life to Begin - Colin Hay
Former lead singer of Men at Work, Oz/Scot Colin Hay from Saltcoats in North Ayrshire articulating a feeling we have all experienced.

5. I Hope You Dance - Lee Ann Womack

One of the benefits of growing old is that you no longer give a hoot how people judge your musical taste. I love country music – next caller.

6. Don't Let Me Be Misunderstood - Lana Del Rey

Recorded by Nina Simone in 1964, a 1965 hit for The Animals and given a twenty-first-century makeover by Lana Del Rey.

7. Something Changed - Pulp

'When we woke up that morning we had no way of knowing/ That in a matter of hours we'd change the way we were going.' Jarvis Cocker

8. Fearless Love - Melissa Etheridge

My pal's dad, Mike Russell, switched me on to Melissa Etheridge blaring through his top-notch hi-fi speakers at Smithfield in the early 1990s.

9. Over the Hillside - The Blue Nile

There is a sorcery that blends listening to the 'The Blue Nile' on a quality hi-fi and drinking Highland Park in the wee small hours. Celtic wizardry.

10. This Mess We're In - PJ Harvey and Thom Yorke

'I didn't want to kiss you goodbye – that was the trouble – I wanted to kiss you goodnight – and there's a lot of difference.' Ernest Hemingway

11. Pavement Cracks - Annie Lennox

'When did we see each other face-to-face? Not until you saw into my cracks and I saw into yours. Before that, we were just looking at ideas of each other, like looking at your window shade but never seeing inside. But once the vessel cracks, the light can get in. The light can get out.' John Green

12. Through Your Hands - John Hiatt
'We scheme about the future and we dream about the past/When just a simple reaching out might build a bridge that lasts.' John Hiatt

13. Protection – Massive Attack (feat. Tracey Thorn)
Everything but the Girl frontwoman Tracey Thorn with Massive Attack – best songs for driving from Leith to Perth at 3.00 a.m. in the morning.

14. Dirty Little Secret - The All-American Rejects
Rock bands from small towns in the USA hold hands with pop and race into the horizon. We all have room for one of these in our playlists.

15. Enjoy the Silence (Single Version) - Depeche Mode
Essex boys from Basildon had us guessing how they made their unique sounds back in Fife, circa 1981. We had a wasp synthesizer.

16. Sometimes Love Just Ain't Enough - Patti Smith (feat. Don Henley)
'I may have hurt you, but I did not desert you/Maybe I just want to have it all.'

17. Cat People (Putting Out Fire) - David Bowie
Bowie and Giorgio Moroder. Critics claimed Bowie was ahead of his time. I never appreciated that until 'Let's Dance' in 1982 – then it made sense.

18. Heartbeats - José González
'To call for hands from above to lean on/Would that be good enough for me?' Karin Dreijer Andersson and Olof Dreijer

19. I Hope that I Don't Fall in Love with You - Tom Waits
'Well the night does funny things inside a man/These old tom-cat feelings you don't understand.' Tom Waits

20. Northern Sky - Nick Drake
'There's this rushing sound, like white noise. The sound of nothing.'
Julia Green

21. Into My Arms - Nick Cave and The Bad Seeds
'That's what people do who love you. They put their arms around you and love you when you're not so lovable.' Deb Caletti

22. Poison and Wine - The Civil Wars
'... your mouth is poison, your mouth is wine.'

23. In Your Eyes - Peter Gabriel
'Almost nothing need be said when you have eyes.' Tarjei Vesaas

24. Sweet Disposition - The Temper Trap
'You're not obligated to win. You're obligated to keep trying. To the best you can do every day.' Jason Mraz

25. Drive - Joe Bonamassa
'Some beautiful paths can't be discovered without getting lost.' Erol Ozan

26. Paper Airplane - Alison Krauss and Union Station
'Our love is like a paper airplane flying in the folded wind, riding high, dipping low.' Robert Lee Castleman

27. Goodbye - Feder (feat. Lyse)
'What is that feeling when you're driving away from people and they recede on the plain till you see their specks dispersing? – it's the too-huge world vaulting us, and it's goodbye. But we lean forward to the next crazy venture beneath the skies.' Jack Kerouac

28. The One That Got Away - The Civil Wars
'I miss the way you wanted me when I was staying just out of your reach.'

19742065R00080

Printed in Great Britain
by Amazon